I0638051

ONE MORE HERO:

THE CASES OF THE FIREBOAT MEN

OTHER BOOKS IN THE
H. BEDFORD-JONES UNIFORM
EDITION LIBRARY:


*The Ghost of Screwface Hanlon*


*Gunpowder Gold*


*The Princess and the Prophet*


*They Lived By the Sword*


*Warriors in Exile*

H . BEDFORD-JONES

# ONE MORE HERO: THE CASES OF THE FIREBOAT MEN

## H. BEDFORD-JONES

ILLUSTRATED BY
LELAND GUSTAVSON

ALTUS PRESS • 2018

© 2018 Altus Press • First Edition—2018

PUBLISHING HISTORY

*One More Hero: The Cases of the Fireboat Men* originally appeared in the July 1938–February 1939 issues of *Blue Book* magazine.

THANKS TO

Everard P. Digges LaTouche and Gerd Pircher

ALL RIGHTS RESERVED

No part of this book may be reproduced or utilized in any form or by any means, electronic or mechanical, without permission in writing from the publisher.

This edition has been marked via subtle changes, so anyone who reprints from this collection is committing a violation of copyright.

Visit altuspress.com for more books like this.

Printed in the United States of America.

# TABLE OF CONTENTS

*Fireboat men must be not only firemen, but
sailors, divers, engineers and police—dangerous
callings, all…. This first story of a colorful series
centers about Gunboat Brendan and the tragic
problem he met below the murky harbor waters.*

**B**ILL BRENDAN was head fireman-diver on Fireboat
Two; but, a man being what his background makes him,
Brendan was more than this.

Everybody in the Los Angeles harbor district knew Gunboat
Brendan, the former Navy boxer, seaman gunner and so forth….
The Navy knew him for his work on sunken submarines; the
fireboat crew knew him for what he was, and Mother Brendan
knew him for what she thought he was. All this was behind his
shoulder now, as he sat hulking over his pipe, listening to the
police broadcast.

"My gosh, boys!" Taylor, the pilot, whistled softly. "Twenty
thousand in currency, and the mugs get away with it. Three of
'em burned down by the cops. The other two steal a parked
patrol car—"

He fell silent, listening. The engineer broke out excitedly.

"Hear that? Headed for the harbor district! Reported by an
officer at Main and Weford; emptied his gun into the car as it
went past, but it kept on."

Brendan nodded soberly, cocking an eye at the window of
the pier office.

"Aint so good. Heavy fog-bank rolling up out o' the west
basin tonight," he observed. "Good night for some drunk to hit
Suicide Curve, too."

The police broadcast ended. There was brisk discussion of
that stolen police car bearing two thugs and a small fortune,

headed now for the harbor. Here at its berth, however, Fireboat Two was in no position to see any possible fun. Suicide Curve, eh?

"That's right," said Taylor solemnly. "About time for another one. Eleven year't I been here, we've fished out sixty-four cars. Harbor Commission's been eleven year waiting to put up stop warnings at those open dead-end streets between the piers. People heading for the ferry terminal in a fog like this had better not be in a rush."

"Remember the family we fished out last winter?" growled

*"Hop to it, you lardos!"*
*shouted Captain Lawrence.*
*"Get those chests over!*
*Move around!"*

Brendan. "That guy was just plain lost. Riles me up whenever I think o' them little tykes drowned, on account of the Harbor Commission saving money. I'd like to be a politician for about ten days."

"You'd make a hot one, all right," jeered the engineer. "You and your—Holy mackerel, listen to that! Talk of the devil, and up he comes!"

The alarm was shrilling. One and all were in motion instantly. A car off the foot of Berth 187, came the shout. A watchman had heard it go off, but knew no details; his alarm had been relayed from headquarters.

Already Fireboat Two was like a swarming beehive. Twenty firemen were loading equipment on the boat's stern, working with precise rapidity. Every instant counted, for there was always the chance of pulling somebody up alive. Not much hope of it tonight, however. This blanketing fog would keep them from getting there in time.

"Hop to it, you lardos!" shouted Captain Lawrence. "Get those chests over. Mike and Johnny, over with the diving ladder. The pump—lower away there!"

Seventy-one seconds after the alarm shrilled, they had the equipment stowed on the wide, flat stern.

Captain Lawrence shot his orders at Duke Dumas, the master-diver.

"Duke! Get Howard dressed for the first dive; slap a suit on Brendan for a stand-by, as usual. Move, you sleepwalkers! This is no pleasure cruise—"

THE CAPTAIN ran forward to where Taylor hung out of the wheel-house, whistle-cord in hand, all three annunciators on *stand-by*. His voice roared:

"All right, all right, men, let's roll! Berth 187. Give her the gun—a car's down. Come on, what's holding us?"

Pilot Taylor tooted the *cast-off* signal. These skippers were all alike, he grumbled audibly; thought a pilot could go speeding upchannel in a pea-soup fog at twenty-five knots, like the rescue wagon from Headquarters. They never seemed to realize that the fireboat master had to feel his way against harbor traffic, sounding his signals according to navigation law and regulating his speed by the same.

"The pilot can't help it," he growled, "if this makes it impossible to get folks up from cars in time. Cars got no business going overboard anyhow." He turned to the engine-room tube as the boat, going slow speed ahead on three engines, emerged from the slip. "Five hundred revs a minute, chief. Dead slow all engines. Keep your crew set for four bells and a jingle astern."

He snapped the speaking-tube shut and took position in the center of the darkened wheel-house, while the Captain cursed softly. "Steer 355 degrees," he instructed the first mate. "Nothing to the west'ard."

"Aye," said the mate, a lean State of Maine mariner. "Three fifty-five and nothing to the west'ard." Peering into the binnacle, he rolled the wheel to port and starboard and settled on his course.

FIREBOAT TWO headed up the channel. Her air-horn tooted at minute intervals, while the watch up forward strained every sense into the woolly wall of fog that hemmed them in. A voice sounded abruptly:

"Beacon Eight dead ahead, skipper! Hear the foghorn on 175, port bow."

"Aye," said Taylor, and changed course at once. Fireboat Two cautiously nosed into Slip Five, and in another minute was alongside Berth 187.

One more minute, and apprentice-diver Howard, in stiff rubber and canvas dress, his domed helmet, hundred-pound waist weights and thirty-pound leaded shoes, was on his way into the pitch-black depths below. Forty feet of water here. An ambulance and a gathering crowd showed on the pier, dimly; so dense was the fog that even the rescue wagon's red light was no more than a dim blur.

Duke Dumas, the master diver in charge, leaned over the

guard-rail, holding the air hose and life-lines. Four men aft at
the pump were turning it over with measured beat, keeping the
pressure at exactly fifteen pounds. Other men tended coils of
life-line and hose, keeping these and the braided telephone-
cable free-running at all times.

The fog swirled eerily. The mist deadened all ordinary sound,
transforming the moving figures into dim wraiths of gigantic
proportions. There was no excitement aboard Fireboat Two.
Under the glaring flood-lights the men went about their work
quietly, efficiently. Many of them had brought Navy discipline
into this job. No undue noise or talk. They were hosemen,
firemen, engineers, paid to fight fire and do rescue work ashore
and afloat; diving duty for sunken cars was nothing novel to
them.

It occasioned far more interest and excitement in the crowd
on the pier—police, land firemen, reporters, morbid gawkers,
watchmen. Most of them knew the procedure and discussed it
as they watched the distorted shapes under the floodlights.

Usually the first diver located the car in the deep mud, made
fast the hook-rope, and signaled topside to break the car out
of the swiftly clutching ooze. Then, his diving-time up, he would
be hauled to the deck, making his report to the battalion chief
in charge. The second, or more experienced diver, would go
down to open the car doors, remove the bodies within, then
bend on the hook-rope preparatory to hoisting the car.

A SHADOWY figure dropped from the pier to the port
side of the deck, where no one was working. Picking his way
over the tangle of gear, he slipped forward to the open door of
the nozzle-room. Inside on a stool towered a monstrous figure
in diving dress, but without the helmet and weights. Brendan
was calmly finishing his pipe, awaiting his turn to go down. He
glanced up in astonished recognition as the visitor came in.

Runt Welch was a waterfront rat of repute as vicious as his
face, twitching that long ratlike nose and staring with blazing
eyes that told their own story. Rumored to be a snowbird and

*"Twenty thousand bucks in a suitcase, see?
We'll get it…. Five grand goes to you."*

dope-peddler, he certainly was not a person Brendan would have expected to see aboard. Welch came in, and with a nod of greeting sat down on an inhalator box.

"Hello, Brendan. Looking for you."

"Like hell." Brendan's scarred, heavy features showed his contempt. "Get out of here before you're kicked ashore."

Welch grinned excitedly. Brendan noted the glassy eyes, the pinpoint pupils. He remembered that he himself was practically helpless while encased in this diving-suit.

"No time to gam." Welch spoke rapidly. "Gunboat, I got a five-thousand-dollar diving-job for you."

Brendan grunted a disdainful laugh. "I don't do commercial diving, Runt. Right now, I'm doing a civilian diver out o' fifty

*Brendan's mind seemed unable to function; he
could think only of Hughie.... "O.K.!" he growled
to the tender, and clumped down the iron ladder.*

bucks by hooking to this car. Aint fair, maybe, but orders is
orders. I hear tell this may be the police wagon stolen after that
hold-up job tonight."

"So it is," said Welch, his eyes agleam.

"Huh? If you know it is, run along and tell the cops."

"I'm telling *you*," snapped Welch. "I drove that car, see? I was
in it. Me and Denver Red. All the others got burned. Then
Denver, he got burned on the way when a cop let go at us as
we passed him. I come down through the fog, missed the turn

and went off the pier. Swum clear to a boat I got waiting, changed my rags, and here I am. Fast work!"

Brendan's blue eyes were wide.

"My God, if you aint all doped up! Why, you blasted little cockroach—"

"Save it, you big stiff," spat out Welch. "I got to talk fast. Twenty thousand bucks in a suitcase, see? Pay-roll made up at the bank; we copped it, sure. It's under the back seat o' that car, Gunboat. When you go down to hook on to the car, you slip out the suitcase and carry it over to one of the pilings; anchor it. You and me—we'll get it tomorrow night with my boat. Five grand goes to you."

Brendan still stared in blank amazement. He knew a dope-fiend when he saw one, and the Runt was obviously all hopped up. The thing was incredible.

"Are you off your nut?" Brendan scowled suddenly. "A cheap rat like you in on a hold-up? Not likely. Chase yourself!"

"Dry up," snapped Welch, leaning forward intently, "Listen here. Denver Red aint been mugged or printed. He aint got a record, see?"

"What's it to me?" snarled Brendan angrily. "Get out of here! You and your orders to me—I don't know if you're crazy or what."

"You'll know damned quick," shot out the other. "I know who Denver Red was, see? And you're doing just what I tell you, Gunboat. You get that suitcase out; then you get Denver out and anchor him too. Then we're all set. Yeah, Denver has told me a lot about you, and about Mother Brendan too."

Brendan took the pipe from his mouth and set it down. He tried to speak and could not. His massive features were suddenly gray, as comprehension came to him. Welch, at these evidences of agitation, uttered a jeering laugh.

"Got the idea, have you? Hughie Brendan—that's him, all right. Your kid brother. And if they pull him up in that car, it's good night! You know what'll happen, what it'll mean, when the story breaks in the papers. It'll dish you and your record. It'll dish her, too. Denver thought a lot o' Mother Brendan, he sure did! Now, you big stiff, you'll do what I tell you. I'll give you a ring later tonight. So behave."

He cocked his head, listening; then suddenly rose, darted out into the fog, and was gone. He had heard some one coming on the run.

Brendan sat there in stark misery, sick of heart and soul, his scarred features agonized, his huge fists clenched, his breath coming fast. Hughie, gone to the bad these two years, vanished, lost! And all the while, Mother Brendan had prayed for him every night and morning, certain he would come back. Well, if this rat spoke truth, he had come back!

IT WAS not of himself or his record that Bill thought; this mattered little. It was of Mother Brendan, and what the story would mean to her.

Probably it was not over thirty seconds that he sat thus; yet his brain moved in the span of days and years. Hughie, for one thing; all the ruined wastrel life of the young fellow. And what this news would mean to the old mother. No pleasant prospect…. Then too there was Welch. The rat's words had unrolled an entire panorama.

A boat waiting here somewhere in the harbor, close by. The pay-roll made up at the bank—yes, all that had come in over the radio broadcast—and Welch acting as driver, probably in charge of the waiting boat and the get-away. Three of the gang shot down. Two away in the stolen police-car, and one of them killed on the mad drive. Welch, going off the dead end in the fog—and below, Hughie Brendan waiting for his brother.

"Come on, Gunboat!" Voices at the door, hasty, excited, jarred through him. "Got to go down. Car's there, but Howard cut his hand on broken glass and didn't get inside. The cops think it may be their car, the one the bandits made a get-away with; probably one or two of 'em are inside now."

AGONY, TERROR, acute horror swept through Gunboat Brendan. Even to move seemed rankly impossible, for his brain was frozen; yet he found himself mechanically rising. Two firemen helped him from the nozzle-room across the deck to another stool. Without a word, he sat while his heavy shoes were laced on.

One of the men was cursing softly; something about volunteer firemen-divers who got no extra pay or merit-marks for going into black depths foul with sunken timbers, cast-off wire hawsers, saw-edged boiler iron and whatnot. Any other time Brendan would have added a curse or two on his own account; but now his mind seemed unable to function. He could only think of Hughie, who had come home again. It was paralyzing.

Lead shoes, lead belt, copper breastplate, then the telephone receivers over his ears. He tested the phones. The helmet was lowered over his head, given a quarter-turn and locked into position. He peered through the glass faceplate, tried his air-valve, tested the exhaust valve, felt for his knife, the wrench, the hanks of light line in his belt; all this done swiftly, automatically.

"O.K.!" he growled to the tender, and clumped down the iron ladder.

No one could tell, thanks to the helmet, that his face was gray and drawn, that his eyes bulged with acute terror behind the thick glass. Had Runt Welch told the truth? There was one way he could be certain. If a suitcase was under the back seat of that car down below, he might be sure the story was true. All sense of sight was ruled out, in the depths. He could see nothing. But the pay-roll suitcase, the same one described in the police radio broadcast, was all the proof he needed.

Groping, Brendan found the car; the touch of it balanced him, heartened him with reality. Here he must work entirely by feel. He got the doors open. He touched the Thing so limply awaiting him, and a sweat of horror bedewed his scarred features. The suitcase was there. The story was true. This limp clay aswing in the water was his brother.

Satisfied of this, he rallied; he knew the worst. Waist-deep in the ooze, he hauled Hughie out. As he lugged the swinging body through the blackness, he could feel the tears on his cheeks. The air hissing through the intake-valve seemed to choke him as he plowed along. Now there was only one thing he could do, and not for his own sake but for that of Mother Brendan. He went grimly ahead with the gruesome, soul-rending job.

For a hundred feet along the wharf, creosoted piling was thrust down into the sand and mud. From his belt Brendan unhooked the light line, cutting off a length with his knife; and by means of this he anchored Hughie to the piling.

He groped his way back to the car and got the heavy suitcase. Back to the piling again; presently he had the suitcase anchored there too. If anything slipped up now, if for any reason a diver came down here tomorrow, he knew full well the implications, and what it would mean to him; but the knowledge did not stagger him. Then he was back at the car again, speaking through the helmet transmitter.

"O.K.! Send down the hook-rope," he told the tender up above. His voice sounded heavy, hoarse. "Ready to send her up. Tell the Chief I've searched the car. Nothing inside except the rear seat cushion floating. No bodies."

When the rope came down and he hooked on, the job was done.

WHEN THEY brought Brendan up, he leaned heavily on the rail while the tenders unlocked and lifted off the helmet. One look at him, and Duke Dumas spoke anxiously.

"You look sick, big boy. What's wrong?"

"I'm a bit off. Must have been something I ate for supper," Brendan replied. "Give me a hand over the rail."

They helped him to the deck, stripped off the clammy suit, wrapped him in blankets and gave him a slug of brandy. He had the shivers, sure enough; they hustled him into Fireboat Three and sent him back to quarters.

After that, Fireboat Two lifted the sunken car with her winch, the eager reporters and police finding it empty. Then, her work done, the boat went hooting back through the fog to her Terminal Island station.

Brendan was still off his feed when the chief looked in on him, so they bundled him into a car and sent him home. For him, home was the Wilmington bungalow where he lived with Mother Brendan.

Half an hour after he got there, the phone rang. Brendan answered the call. At sound of Welch's thin and squeaky voice, he shivered again and felt sweat on his face.

"Aye," he said grimly. "Everything done. Tomorrow night? It's my shift off; yes."

He listened. Welch had the boat made ready for the gang; he, the sole survivor, was now heir to all their preparations. He, out of all those five men, alone was living. And Gunboat Brendan knew that he himself must now depend on this cheap crook, this contemptible scoundrel of the waterfront.

"I'll get everything and send it to the boat, aye," he said. "You've marked the piles, you say? All right, you can depend on me. Will there be fog tomorrow night, you say? Sure. Every night for a week, now."

So it was settled.

NEXT EVENING, fog was again rolling in past the Point. The battleships inside the breakwater were sounding "At anchor" signals, and the giant bell that some authority had placed near Fireboat Two's berth was tolling its nerve-shattering warning, its voice fairly shaking the quarters of the boat crew. There would be no sleep for the boys this night.

Gunboat Brendan, on his regular off shift, was ready for the dreaded job. Near midnight, a little fishing-boat left its moorings at the landing near the yacht club, and cautiously felt its way down the channel to Slip Five. In the boat lay a helmet

and oxygen jacket Brendan had bought that day from "Suicide" Svenson's widow. Svenson had lost his life going after a fouled dredge anchor off the new breakwater extension. Brendan figured he could use the outfit himself, later.

"Did you read about the job in the papers?" Brendan asked.

Welch grunted.

"Sure thing. Lucky they blasted them three mugs good and proper; nobody's left to squeal about me and your brother. Somebody had tipped off the cops and they were all set for the mob."

"Who did the talking?" Brendan inquired and the other swore viciously.

"I dunno. Monk Hawley had a moll. I dope it that she was sore on him and phoned in a tip to the cops. Can't tell."

Brendan sensed suspicion, defiance, distrust, in the manner of Welch, who pointedly kept him beyond arm's reach. He accepted the situation without argument, intent solely upon what now lay ahead. A man is what his background makes him;

*Brendan grunted: "I didn't go to do that, confound it! No help for it now, though. And no harm done the world, either!"*

Brendan's one and only thought at the moment was back in the bungalow where, this same night, Mother Brendan prayed for the return of Hughie.

THE FISHING-BOAT crept into Slip Five, with Brendan forward and Welch at the helm. She made fast to the piling where Fireboat Two had lain the previous night. Not a soul moved on the pier, no ship or tug navigated the fog-bound channel. Welch was a long time in finding the particular piles he had marked the night before, but at last he found them, and came down the ladder from the dock platform.

"All set. The watchman's asleep in his doghouse, as usual. We're O.K., if some other darn' fool don't come along and run his car off. Ready?"

"Yeah," grunted Brendan. He sent down a shot line to the bottom. Hughie would be there, within a few feet of it. Then he got out the diving jacket and helmet.

"Now, listen," he said. "It aint so hot working in one of these gadgets at forty feet. If I get fouled, down there, I'm liable to stay with Hughie. You handle your end of the job right, or we're all sunk together."

"Shoot, and don't waste time," said Welch impatiently. "This fog is cold as hell."

"So's the water down below," Brendan countered grimly. Even in the fog and dark, he suspected from Welch's position that the smaller man was holding a pistol. "First, I'll get up my brother's body. Then, after the suitcase comes up, I want to use this boat. I'll go out while the fog's heavy and bury Hughie in deep water off the Point."

"Sure, sure, you can have the damned boat, and five grand besides," snarled Welch. He did not move from where he stood. "Get on with the job."

Brendan indicated the shot line. "See this line? I go down on it, taking the heaving line with me. You hang on to the heaving line from topside. Better come forward and take it now, and keep it running free. In the cockpit it's apt to get fouled."

As he spoke, he flaked out the heaving line on the little fo'c'sle. It was dark up forward; the fog was thicker than ever, swirling around him, distorting his figure out of all proportion. The deck was wet and slippery, filmed with fish oil and the grease of years.

Welch peered at him intently but did not move.

"I'm staying here till you go down," he rejoined decisively. His hand jerked up a bit; Brendan was certain now that he held a gun. "Don't you try to pull nothing on me, Gunboat. I aint trusting you a whole lot."

"Oh, don't be a damned fool—"

Brendan swung around. His feet slipped and went out from under him. He fell with a crash, half against the little wheelhouse. A groan escaped him, as he lay in a twisted heap. Welch's voice shrilled with alarm.

"Hey! What's the matter with you?"

Brendan moved, tried to claw himself up, and fell back with a subdued oath.

"Can't make it. Can't get up. Must have twisted my back. Come here and give me a hand, you rat!"

Welch cursed softly, viciously. "You big lummox, to go hurt yourself at a time like this! You're pulling something. I got a mind to blast you right now."

"And bring everybody down on us? You're no such fool." Brendan laughed harshly. "Why you damned cokehead, I'm just as anxious as you are to get this done! My kid brother's down there with the crabs eating on him. I can't get him buried without your help, and you know it. Come on, damn you, give me a hand!"

"I guess you're right." Welch moved forward, reluctantly. "Where you hurt?"

"It's my back. Jammed against the wheel-house, here; I can't seem to get on my feet." Brendan twisted again, and once more relaxed with a low gasp. "Confound it all! If I could just get up on my legs, I'd be all right. This deck's an inch thick with slime. Come on, get your hands under my shoulders and lift, will you? I'm stuck here."

HIS SUSPICION dissipated, Welch came and stood over the big, helpless figure. He leaned down, got his hands under Brendan's arms, and pulled. Brendan groaned.

"It hurts, but it helps. Get a better grip, now, and we'll make it."

Welch obeyed. His hands well under Brendan's arms, he stooped to tug upward.

Of a sudden, Brendan's arms clamped in with tremendous pressure, pinioning Welch's wrists. A sharp yelp broke from

Welch. He lost balance. The gun escaped his fingers. He clutched frantically at Brendan—and yelped again as he fell.

The two figures thrashed confusedly about the little deck, under a swirl of thick fog. Twice more little convulsive yelps broke from Welch, like the squeaks of a cornered rat. Then came a subdued, thudding crash…. Presently Brendan scrambled to his feet.

N O   A L A R M .  The sleeping watchman had heard nothing. The little boat rocked quietly under the fog. Brendan stooped to feel the limp figure at his feet, and grunted.

"I didn't go to do that, confound it! No help for it now, though. If his neck broke, he deserved it a dozen times over. And no harm done the world, either,"

He turned calmly to the equipment. He laced on the heavy lead shoes and donned the diving jacket and helmet; this light, shallow-water equipment would do in such a pinch. He made his preparations with unhurried care. Gunboat Brendan always took one thing at a time and made sure it was right before going ahead. No more need to worry about Runt Welch, at least. Now to keep the rendezvous with Hughie; no earthly pay would have tempted him to undertake what he was about to do for love.

Gingerly, he lowered himself down the knotted shot line into the oily water. Never had his huge gnarled paws stood him in better stead than on this night, or done grimmer work. Once in the blackness, acute fear struck him. Never before had he gone down without tenders watching above. Now, if the least thing went wrong in the gripping ooze, he was lost.

Better so, however, than with Runt Welch waiting to kill him, after the suitcase was recovered. He had cherished no illusions regarding that man's intent.

Even in this moment of gnawing revulsion and fear, he could not repress a grim smile that curled his battered lips like a snarl, and a twisted thought that came into his brain slantwise. Once he had heard a frenetic soapbox orator blaspheming about "God's jokes." The phrase crept upon his mind. God's jokes!

Well, this was one, and no mistake. If only Runt Welch had known the truth!

His outstretched hands came upon the floating, anchored Thing, and he shivered....

When he had made fast his lines to corpse and suitcase, he went back topside with the hiss of the oxygen fretting his senses. No tenders, no helpers over the side. Swirls of fog blacker than ever. He might have cast off his heavy weighted shoes, but Brendan was a practical man, and this equipment had value. He felt his way up the line; those big knotted hands of his accomplished the impossible.

At length, trembling with exhaustion, he was aboard. He rid himself of the outfit and lay gathering his forces. Then he rose on the slippery deck and fell to work. The worst of it was over, anyhow.

He brought in the stiff, streaming figure and the suitcase, all its seals intact. From the fo'c'sle of the boat he dragged some old canvas. Impartially, he swathed Welch and the other in this canvas. Before finishing, he secured Welch's flashlight and stole just one glimpse of the face from the depths. The recognition of Hughie steeled him to all he had done and still must do.

He bound the two wrapped bodies around and around with lobster-pot lines.

At Hughie's feet he secured the boat's anchor. Then he lifted the slippery suitcase into the wheel-house, took out his diving-knife, and slit one side of the wet leather. He felt inside and brought out a number of pieces of metal, and flashed the light on them.

"Washers! Washers and junk!" he muttered grimly. "Those cops around the boat, last night, sure told the truth. Lucky thing it never got into the newspapers, or Welch would have seen about it. A decoy suitcase! The holdup had been tipped off, of course. A decoy suitcase, and five men dead because of it! Oh, Hughie boy—"

He checked back his threatening emotion. Lugging the

suitcase out again, he made it fast to the limp bundle that was Runt Welch. One of God's jokes, sure enough, he told himself.

Then, starting the motor, he cast off.

AT THE entrance of Slip Five, he took his departure from Beacon Eight and headed down the main channel toward the Point, He passed Fireboat Two. The B-platoon boys would be playing cards down below, he knew, trying to dull their senses to the damning toll of the giant fog-bell so close beside. That bell dinned its unending solemn dirge as he thrummed past and away into the fog, heading for Barracuda Flats and the two-hundred-fathom depth that would close the story.

And Mother Brendan would go on with her prayers, in blessed ignorance.

# DOGHOUSE BLUES

*A strange waterfront drama comes to its*
*climax in a scene of flaming hazard*

BLAKE SAT before Rosie Vidiano's lunch-counter, ate his meal unhurriedly, and looked often at Rosie Vidiano. She was good to look upon, with her sparkling vitality, her gold-bronze mop of hair, her trim feminine allure. Blake knew her story—a bride of a month, her husband killed in the Terminal Warehouse fire. Now she supported herself and her young brother by this lunch-counter.

She came over to him for a moment, with her swiftly flashing smile.

"What are you doing in this part of town? Haven't seen you for so long—"

"That wasn't my fault," Blake rejoined. "You're going to see a lot of me from now on, Rosie. I'm reporting at two o'clock to the *Viking.*"

Her face changed. Her eyes probed him sharply with dismayed incredulity.

"No!" she exclaimed. "You're joking. Not you—oh, it can't be true!"

Blake nodded. "On my way down and out? Maybe so, maybe not. Where's the kid?"

"Jimmy? At school. Do you know Ironhead? He's coming up the street."

"Sure. We entered the department together."

She nodded and moved off. Blake's gaze followed her warmly....

Outside beneath a hot sun lay the long, shabby road with its sooty dock-sheds on one hand, and on the other its dingy seamen's hotels, cheap-john stores and dance-halls. Far as the eye could reach, north and south, were berthed the tramps of the sea, spewing forth brown laughing men with rings in their ears, dignified dark men with caste-marks, furtive yellow men, bold, boasting white men: officers, firemen, deck-hands, longshoremen. And Rosie Vidiano, earning a living with a smile amid all these tongues of Babel, but with never a salty oath along her counter. Men who knew no better were soon taught their manners by other men.

The door opened, and Captain Murphy tramped in—Ironhead Murphy. His bulk filled the little entrance. He shoved back the cap from his massive features.

"Ha, Rosie! Eggs and beans and a kiss for a fire-chief, lass!"

"You'll get the kiss when you've got the chief's badge, Cap'n," she rejoined.

BLAKE MET the hot eyes of Murphy, and nodded greeting.

"So here you are, fire-prevention engineer!" jeered Murphy. "Thought you were to report this morning, Blake?"

"Two o'clock's the orders," said Blake coolly, and jerked a thumb toward the clock on the wall.

"Then make it to the minute, or your record's off to a bad start on its last lap," growled Murphy; and planted himself at the counter without further regard. Blake flushed slightly. Last lap, eh? True enough. He could fully comprehend the dismay in Rosie's eyes at hearing he had been transferred to the *Viking*.

And as he finished his meal, as his quiet, searching gaze touched here and there, he could comprehend that Murphy knew a good thing when he saw it—and that Rosie Vidiano did not wholly appreciate the flattering attentions. When Blake paid his check at the front end, he looked into Rosie's eyes for an instant.

"I'll be seeing you," he said quietly. She made change, lifted her gaze to his.

"It won't be hard," was her brief reply; and what he read in her face was enough to bring out his quick smile.

Thoughtfully, he went on to the end of the street, a hefty figure of a man though lacking Murphy's obvious brawn. Ahead of him loomed the Doghouse, once a ferry terminal but now a fireboat station, where the *Viking* berthed.

THE TWO new fire-tugs could handle ordinary hazards along the waterfront. Only when gigantic work lay ahead was the *Viking* called in, with her powerful six-thousand-gallon pumps. Usually hers was the ignoble task of pumping out sunken barges and other craft after the new boats had flooded the fire in them.

The Doghouse quartered the crews of the *Viking*, Foamite Company No. 4, and the spare triple-combination all-service rig; and Ironhead Murphy was kingpin here. Like most of his men, he had originally been sent here for punishment; unlike most, he had stayed on, becoming an asset instead of a liability to the department.

Murphy had a free hand here; the battalion chief seldom visited Engine 72, as the Doghouse was officially known. Murphy was a brute. He was not efficient, but he was a master at ramrodding the men sent him—booze-fighters, department deadbeats, gold-bricks, inepts, insubordinates. Here was the jumping-off place, sometimes literally. Out of the service or overboard or back to a steadier job. Headquarters cared little which exit the Doghouse crew took, and breathed freer for having Murphy on hand.

When a man landed in the Doghouse, he was on his way out, with odds-on betting that he would not last till next payday. Murphy, surprisingly enough, put many a "finished" man back into the service; but he was not loved.

Blake looked over the place—rickety, dirty, with a rusting hulk of a fireboat that defied the efforts of fifteen men to keep her clean, and a hard-boiled captain who defied his fifteen men not to keep her clean. Every large fire department has its "doghouse"—its remote companies where useless men wait until authority has enough on them for a discharge under the civil-service regulations.

AT T W O o'clock, to the second, Blake walked into the foul den of an office. Murphy cocked a hard eye at him.

"So you got enough reverse seniority to make the Doghouse, huh?"

"It's a revelation," drawled Blake. "I never believed such a place could exist in the department. Looks like a hogpen and smells like a monkey-cage."

"It'll smell worse now, with a firebug around. Making money on the side, eh?" Murphy grinned wickedly when he saw Blake

*"So here you are, fire-prevention engineer!" he jeered.
"Thought you were to report this morning, Blake?"*

go white at the thrust. "You're not the first slicker to make
money out of his job. Oh, I know it's not proved on you! But I
say what I damned please. And you say 'sir' when you address
me. You're not in your palsy-walsy Fire Prevention Bureau now.
We got discipline here."

"Looks like it," sneered Blake. "Rats too, apparently. And
bats in the hose-tower and in your own belfry. Don't kid me,
Ironhead. We came on the job together."

"We won't leave together." Murphy siphoned a stream of

tobacco-juice at a long-neglected spittoon. "You'll go first, with a can tied to your tail. And I saw you making sheep's-eyes at Rosie a while back. Lay off, or your neck will be broke; she's my property. And watch your step around here, firebug."

"Watch your tongue," Blake said quietly. "You lay that name to me before one witness, and I'll have you jerked up so hard you'll leave a vacancy in this soft berth. And lay it to me once more in private if you want to go to the hospital. Right now."

Murphy regarded him with a grin. "Nope. Nothing's proved on you; I'll wait till it is. Now change clothes and turn to. Your station is the nozzle-room, and that takes in the water-tower."

"That's the job for new men, Murphy!" Blake spoke in astonishment. "I'm an engineer and—"

"So far as I'm concerned, you're a rookie. You've been in fire-prevention so long you don't know a Gleeson valve from a circulating nozzle. But you'll learn, so ditch your dude outfit and turn to. I make inspection at ten. The man whose station aint up to snuff stands floor-watches all day and does the evening K.P. Beat it now; and mind one thing you've forgotten. What is it?"

Blake nodded. "Very well, sir."

W E L L   F O R   him that of late he had been bitterly schooled in self-control; he was white to the lips as he went his way. "She's my property—" The blatant, lying words burned into him, all the more because he knew them to be lying words. And he knew that Ironhead Murphy would make life hell for him here, unless he did keep his self-control. Firebug, eh? He had nearly slipped the leash at that word, but Murphy had backed down.

In the nozzle-room, he grimaced. This rectangular compartment abaft the pilothouse was a mess. The night before, or the week before, had seen a fire; everything was greasy and corroded with salt water. Enough work here to keep three men busy all day.

There were rows of ponderous three-and-a-half inch shut-offs and nozzles weighing sixty pounds, which could only be handled by half a dozen men with a hundred pounds of pressure on the hose-line. There were rows of two-and-a-half inch nozzles, and in front of these the handier metro inch-and-a-half nozzles.

Blake surveyed the Siamese connections used to make many smaller lines from one large hose; a dozen of them, all sizes. Reducers, adapters, spanners, sprinkler shut-offs, circulating nozzles, deck and rail standees for securing and holding the big pipes under high pressure during long hours of cooling down the ashes of a dock or building. Here were the smoke-mask boxes with their hoses, air pumps, leather helmets for use in smoky ships' holds. Ponderous Gleeson valves, with intricate machinery for controlling water-pressure between the pumps and hose-lines. Crowbars, sledges, hose-straps, shallow-water diving pump and whatnot, all mingled in one indescribable tangle.

Over everything hung the musty smell of old smoke. The canvas turn-out coats in the lockers had seen many fires, and no one thought of airing them. Limp on their hooks, eaten away by acids, burned by cinders, spotted by oil, chemicals and salt water, the names of forgotten firemen stenciled across their backs, they were mute testimony to neglect. Over them hung battered helmets, the property of anyone who got here first after the alarm came in, their black front pieces starred with the legend: "*Fireboat Viking, Engine 72.*"

Blake hung up his own outfit and pitched into the seemingly hopeless job.

"Discipline, eh? Serves me right," he muttered, pausing to rest after half an hour which had effected little to the eye. "I should have resigned. But I'll stay in this junk-pile and fight it out. Lord, what a mess! What junk!"

"Junk!" came an echoing voice.

He looked up. Framed in the starboard door was a fantastic figure limply hung with old garments, a burlap sack over its

*"You know how kids are—sooner monkey
around with junk, than eat! George the
Slav tells Jimmy stories by the hour."*

shoulder, a heavy cane in one arthritis-twisted claw. George the
Slav, a junky.

"Hello, George!" grunted Blake in surprise. "What are you
doing here? Thought your beat lay uptown?"

George the Slav rattled his stick. "Not any more. Gimme
some junk!"

"Plenty of junk here, all right, but not for you." And Blake
laughed. "Better scram before Cap'n Murphy sees you."

"Yah! I know Murphy. I know you, too. Sp'iled my business
uptown, you did." The unshaven lips twisted in a grimace. "No
more junk in the alleys for George. No more business. Now I
come here and find you. Yah!"

HE TURNED away and disappeared disgustedly. Blake flung an uneasy oath after him, and fell to work again, frowning.

George the Slav, eh? That junky was his evil genius, and hated him bitterly, like every other junky in the city; this was part of the job of fire-prevention engineer. He had cleaned up alleys and back-yards and cellars, removing trash and debris; and in obviating fire-hazards he had spoiled business for the nameless, furtive wretches who flit from alley to alley. Not that their hatred worried him. It was odd to find George the Slav over here in the waterfront district, however.

To Blake's suspicious astonishment, Ironhead Murphy came along on inspection, grunted on surveying the place, and walked out without comment. There was a certain decency to the man, thought Blake; a certain justice. He would make life hell for this new member of the Doghouse crew, but he would do it in his own way.

Blake was right about this. When, a couple of days later, he dropped in at Rosie Vidiano's lunch-counter for coffee and doughnuts, there was a grim set to his jaw that told its own story. The place chanced to be empty.

"You look as if you'd been working," she said, inspecting him. Blake smiled.

"I have. It'll do me good, maybe."

"I've heard stories," she told him flatly, and looked him in the eye. "I'd be interested in learning the truth. You're the last person I'd think to see in the Doghouse."

Blake looked at her. "Interested? Well, you're the one person I'd like to have know the truth. Who's been talking to you?"

"Never mind," she said. "And no kidding, now. How does a fire-prevention engineer get into the Doghouse?"

"By setting fires," he retorted grimly. "Clearing up fire hazards is a tough job. More'n one man wearing a badge has picked up soft dough by calling a dirty spot clean and non-hazardous."

"Not you," she said laconically.

Blake's hard, direct gaze softened.

"Thanks. I did raise hell cleaning things up for a while. Then fires began to break out right along in places I had called clean—and they *were* clean. The insurance people put their experts on the job. The arson-squad worked overtime. All they could find was that some of those fires had been set deliberately. A lot of folks in the industrial district haven't made money and weren't a bit sore to rake in some insurance; but nothing could be pinned on anyone. Looked like somebody was in league with somebody else, and somebody who knew all the dodges, too."

"Why would they pick you?" she demanded, watching him intently.

"Plenty of reasons," Blake said. "It had to be somebody who knew every blind alley and rat-hole and basement, and where fires could be set and remain undetected till they got a roaring start. Somebody who knew where chemicals were stored, what was in the basements and storerooms."

"They wouldn't pick a man in the department without reason," she said in her blunt way.

BLAKE SHRUGGED. "Anonymous letters; somebody had it in for me. They shadowed me and got nowhere. But I was on the spot. When they looked into my bank-account and found it was fat, they just jumped. No proof, of course; they just sent me to the Doghouse, hoping I'd resign. Too many firemen have gone into the incendiary business when off duty. Too easy to draw down a cut from interested parties. Well, I'm here, and I'm staying; and by the Lord, I'll land the right guy one of these days!"

"Who? Who do you think?"

"Can't suspect a soul, Rosie."

"Where'd you get the money?"

Blake met her direct gaze again. "Race track—and I couldn't prove it. My cousin's a trainer and sends me tips. I've picked up quite a little coin that way. They wouldn't believe it, and claimed I had merely covered up. Satisfied?"

She put her hand across the counter. "Shake. I like you."

"That goes double," Blake said quietly. "I've liked you a long time, Rosie."

"Don't be a fool." She jerked her hand away, flushing a little. "Customers coming in, too. If I pick up any loose talk, I'll let you know."

Blake finished his coffee and paid for his meal. "Where's the kid? This is Saturday."

"He went off with George the Slav. He likes the junky, and George likes him." She shrugged. "You know how kids are— sooner monkey around with junk than eat! I guess the old buzzard is safe enough. He tells Jimmy stories by the hour. I've watched 'em."

Her tone told Blake plenty. If she had watched them, she had missed nothing. If she had concluded that George was harmless, she was right. His admiration for Rosie Vidiano went up a notch. That girl had brains.

Blake went back to work, wondering who had talked to her about him. Murphy, no doubt; it was an open secret that Murphy was courting Rosie Vidiano. Her name did not recur between the two men, but there were black looks enough.

AS TIME wore on, as days passed in to weeks, the black looks grew into blacker words that boded ill. Sooner or later an explosion was coming, and the crew awaited it with gleeful anticipation. That the two men were deep and bitter enemies was evident to all hands, and not to them alone.

The boy Jimmy, when not in school, spent much of his time aboard the boat or in the office. He was a boon companion with the men, who relished his boyish impudence; even the dour Ironhead relaxed in his company, gamming with him by the hour. Blake, who had formerly been fast friends with Jimmy, fancied that the boy was avoiding him, until one day Jimmy suddenly showed up in the nozzle-room where Blake was at work alone.

"Hi, stranger!" said Blake cheerfully. "Where you been keeping yourself lately?"

"Nosing around." Jimmy regarded him with serious mien. "Look here, Blake: you and me are friends, aren't we?"

"We've been friends a long while, Jimmy. Are you in a jam?"

"No, but you are," said the boy unexpectedly. "Say, I've heard a lot of talk, and Sis let out something about people setting fires and so forth. I bet a dollar I know who's been doing you dirt."

B L A K E  G A V E him a quick glance.

"Who?"

"Well, I been running around with George the Slav quite a lot. He's a regular guy most of the time, but he takes queer streaks—"

"And you'd better lay off him, son."

"Aw, I can take care of myself," said Jimmy. "But all of those junkies hate you like poison, see? Your fire-prevention work hit 'em under the belt, honest; and what you started, the department keeps up. They blame you for doing 'em out of business, and they got some kind of association that talks things over. Yes sir, I'll bet anything that they're the ones who are after you! I'm keeping my ears open, and I'll find out something about who's been setting fires, you see! Maybe it's George himself, only I hardly think he'd do that. He was the son of a noble back in the old country, and he's told me a lot about it."

Blake nodded. "Well, Jimmy, thanks a lot! By thunder, it makes me feel good to have a friend like you around! You may be dead right about the junkies; that's occurred to me, but of course I couldn't prove anything. Still, I hate to have you running around with those birds. You should be in better company."

"Well, I got reasons, and that makes it okay," said the beaming Jimmy. He turned to leave, then paused. "I hate to break bad news to you, partner, but I got to do it: Ironhead has it in for you, all right. He's going to make you acting captain, to rule the Doghouse when he has his day off. So long, and good luck!"

With a wave of the hand, he was gone.

Acting captain, eh? This news drove Jimmy's hypothesis about the fires being set by junkies and blamed on him, clear out of Blake's mind. And when, an hour later, he was actually detailed as acting captain, he did not set it to any warped sense of justice on Murphy's part. Far from it.

As the days passed, he was confirmed in his belief. Murphy had simply saddled him with a killing detail that would be certain to get him in bad with all hands.

Blake went at the entire boat in the same manner he had tackled the nozzle-room, aiming at clean efficiency. He worked the men hard, and they came to hate him. Expecting this, he accepted it grimly. When he had his chance to fight a blaze, he did it with such efficiency that the battalion chief was jubilant, and made the remark that Blake did a better job than Murphy. This remark was like oil flung on a fire.

The growls and ill-will passed beyond words. Fighting in the department was punished by dismissal, and therefore it never occurred, but black eyes began to appear aboard. They were gained in mysterious ways. Blake's big knuckles began to be barked all the time. Visiting firemen grinned at the black eyes and tipped winks; but Blake kept his mouth shut. Somewhere, somehow, a blow-off must come—everyone knew it.

Business, meantime, was picking up, as fires recurred with regularity. Each time Blake had a day off, that same night a blaze hit somewhere in the district. He saw Rosie from time to time, but seldom ran into Jimmy; probably the boy had forgotten his impulsive endeavor to discover anything, he re-flected, and it was just as well.

He knew that suspicion was fingering him, and that he was being shadowed whenever off duty. He played no more race-track tips, and had every moment of his time accounted for,

*"Aboard the boat—everybody!" shouted Blake.*

watching himself and everyone around him like a hawk. None the less, fires increased in the waterfront district, and the strain began to be almost past bearing.

O N  A  Saturday evening, his off day, Blake came back from downtown. Outside Rosie's lunch-counter he came face to face with Murphy.

"You're in charge tomorrow," said Ironhead. "I'm going fishing."

"Suits me." Blake met the hard gaze with his own hard gaze. "What's biting at your alleged brain? You look like you were trying to think."

"I was just wondering where the blaze will be tonight or tomorrow," retorted Murphy significantly. "And who'll come

aboard with black eyes tomorrow.... I know your mark, Blake. I know you like to tap an eye and leave it black."

"There's a pair of eyes I'd like to tap," Blake said. "It'd be not one but two shiners the dirty louse would be wearing if he ever invited me into that old shed to look at the spiles there."

Murphy's big jaw set hard. "Aye, like enough; if he was an officer, you'd just love to get a black mark on his record! But he'd be too smart for you. He could lick the pants off you with one hand and make a ruin of that big nose of yours to boot."

"Talk's cheap." Blake grinned. "If you're all through spouting, I want to go in and get my supper. I've some business with Rosie."

"I've warned you once," said Murphy in a low, intent voice.

"This is a nice public place if you're not afraid to argue the matter."

"To hell with you!" snapped Ironhead Murphy, and stamped away. He was not letting himself in for any fight with the whole town looking on.

CHUCKLING, BLAKE settled himself at the lunch-counter and ordered supper. When the chance offered, Rosie came and arranged the counter in front of him. She looked him in the eye as she shifted the salt and sauce about.

"Two men were in here awhile ago," she said then. "Strangers. Looked like under-cover guys to me. They talked in Italian; and my folks were Italian."

Blake tensed to the look in her eyes. "Thank God and your folks that you're what you are, Rosie!" he said smilingly. "I wouldn't have you one bit different for the world. When are you going to listen to me?"

"Shut up, you fool; this is important," she said, drawing back a little as he touched her hand. "They'd been asking questions about you, at the slip. Somebody got another of those letters you mentioned to me. The fire-chief himself, I think it was. Saying you had boasted you were going to set a blaze this afternoon or tonight that would bring out every boat in the harbor."

Blake whistled softly. "Hello! My unknown friend is getting crude," he said. "So they were trying to find out whether I'd been talking to any of the crew and boasting of my firebug exploits! As if I'd be such a fool! Headquarters must be jittery."

"You'd better run down. the firebug who's really at work," she said earnestly. "Tell me: who hates you so much?"

"Well, I've got lots of unfriendly faces around, for a fact," he answered soberly. "Lord! This is important and no mistake. I can't thank you enough, Rosie. I'll keep an eye open, you bet. Remember, girl, tonight we have a date for a movie—"

"No," she said. "Tonight, you keep an eye open! This is important."

"But I'm on duty tomorrow night—"

"Never mind. We'll make it Monday, or the first night you're free," she said firmly. "The big thing now is for you to get cleared up with your job."

"Okay. And when are you going to listen to me—seriously?"

"The minute you're reinstated and cleared."

"You mean it? Is that a promise?"

"And not one minute before," she added; but as she departed, the smile she flung over her shoulder brought joyous warmth to Blake's eyes.

H E   W A S   on tenterhooks that night, but nothing happened. No alarm came in. Blake sat around the quarters with the crew, got into a card game, and the evening passed. As he later learned, a throng of police and under-cover men were about the whole district that evening, thanks to the anonymous warning; and nothing happened. When the pilot finally went aboard the Viking and tumbled into his bunk, Blake followed suit.

No alarm that night. Nothing happened Sunday. Ironhead was gone fishing, and Blake was in charge, and it was a dull, hot day, with the white sunlight burning the old docks and rickety warehouses to tinder. All ready for a spark, morosely thought Blake, and he savagely kept his men busy.

Evening found him reading the paper in the captain's office, while the men gammed or played cards. Suddenly the door opened and the pilot came in, with a disgusted look.

"Here's Ironhead, and drunk, with a bag o' fish. Who the devil wants fish!"

Murphy it was, dumping a sack on the floor.

"Mackerel, yellertail, tuna," he sang out boisterously, then quieted as he caught the stare of Blake. "Oh! Blake, I want a word with you. Private. Come outside."

Blake nodded, joined him, and they went out to the street.

Murphy halted and jerked a thumb at the deserted shed adjoining.

"How's it look to you? I s'pose you had nothing to do with Rosie turning down the fish I brought her, huh?"

"Are you crazy? Or just plain drunk?" snapped Blake. "What are you talking about?"

"You know, blast you!" exclaimed the other in a fury. "She wouldn't have 'em. Said she was able to buy her own. Your doin's, you damn' lunkhead! And I s'pose—"

It dawned on Blake that the skipper was actually drunk.

"I'm on duty and responsible," he said curtly. "Go home and sober up."

But Murphy's fist met the side of his jaw and knocked him reeling, to bring up against the wall.

"How about it now? Dark enough to suit you?" jeered Ironhead. His jeer ended in a gasp, as Blake came into him with a rush. The street was dark, empty, deserted, for it was close to eight o'clock.

Perhaps two minutes later, Ironhead Murphy collapsed for the third time.

"If you weren't drunk, I'd give you the shiners I promised," rasped Blake. "I'll do that tomorrow when you're worth taking on. Right now, you pull yourself up and—"

He swung around suddenly and stepped out from the building into the lighted street, as he heard his name called. A figure was running toward him.

"Rosie! What's wrong?" he demanded.

"Thank heaven!" she gasped out, clutching at him, unaware of Murphy, scrambling in the shadows. "Jimmy's gone, with him—you've got to get busy! Jimmy left a note for me—"

Blake suddenly froze, gripped her arm with such force that a cry of pain escaped her. A long shrill ringing came from the Doghouse. She began to speak, and he hushed her with a sharp word. The staccato identifying-signal was coming in over the alarm signal—One! One-two-three! One-two-three-four! And repeated three times.

"Box 134, Front and Dock—why, it's right here!" Blake wheeled. Looking up the street, he could see a figure at the alarm box under the arc-light. The old bent watchman from Pier Two, sending in a second alarm. "Pier Two, Rosie— that means your stand will go up! Clean out everything valuable—"

"Wait, wait!" She caught at him, screaming. Blake had a brief glimpse of Murphy's figure, staggering for the Doghouse entrance. Everything had passed in a flash of time, it seemed.

"I'm trying to tell you—Jimmy's gone there, with him! With George the Slav—Jimmy left a note about it. Suspected something wrong—"

"I've got to go," snapped Blake. "I'll see about it—do what I can. Good God, Pier Two's full of shellac and scrap rubber!"

He was gone with a rush.

MURPHY WAS on the afterdeck, helmet over his ear, roaring maudlin oaths. Blake leaped to the fireboat's rail and darted forward. The pilot was anxiously leaning out of the wheelhouse door, and yelled at him:

"Where to? That damn' fool Murphy's drunk as a hoot-owl. I'll conk him with a spanner if he comes in here, Where to, dammit?"

"Take it easy," rejoined Blake. "Pier Two—right on top of us. Ah, there she goes! Get going, for the love of Mike!"

Fire had suddenly leaped into the night sky. Blake watched; through his brain the words of Rosie jangled with engine-room jangles, vibrated with the full speed ahead throb of the engines. The pilot was yelling to the men to cast off, Murphy was shouting furious orders—no time to think now of anything but duty. Fire came first.

Blake found himself beside the furious Murphy, gripping him into attention.

"I'm in charge. Belay or I'll give you more of the same! Take charge of the hose if you want to get in on this with me—are we together or do I go to work on you?"

"Fire comes first, damn you," said Murphy. Curious, thought Blake, how the man had caught the very words out of his brain. "Okay, Blake…. I'm all right now."

The pilot was bawling to the mate, at the wheel. "Hard starboard—ease her now; steady! We'll go alongside that standpipe under Door 35."

"Aye." The mate peered ahead at the smoke in the slip, and the leaping flames above.

"Port a spoke—so! Steady as you go!"

The *Viking* surged down the slip, her stack belching. Half-speed now as the pilot rang down the annunciator. Back came the answering jangle.

"Hey, Blake!" shouted the pilot. "Fenders and grapnels—ready? Stand by, then. All right—heave!" He swung back to the mate. "Hard over—port!" The twin annunciators went to "full astern." The boat vibrated and her ancient engines jumped in their bedplates as the headway was killed and she came to rest. The pilot went to the pump annunciator in the after end of the wheelhouse and rang for two hundred pounds pressure.

"All right, out you go!" he told the mate.

Blake had taken charge in the nozzle room and now came out on deck with swift orders.

Murphy had subsided, now, and the hose was coming out.

"Bend on two Gleesons to two Sections of three-and-a-half inch. Put six shut-offs on the manifolds, port and starboard. Two of you aloft in the tower—train your stream where you see the most fire. Two more for'ard and two aft on the monitors. Another on the wheelhouse. Work together, now, use your heads! Pilot, stand by to shift around bows on, if we have to work it that way."

Suddenly everything was moving like a well-oiled machine. Fifty-foot sections of hose were run to the dock, the brass nozzles on. Quicker than speech, training had taken effect, muscles had reacted, the men were on the job like one. Water towers were up, pouring their streams on the bright spots amid the smoke. The deck monitors fore and aft, handled like guns by their two-man crews, shot in their full force. But smoke and flame and cinders rocketed skyward from the hell-broth on the pier.

"She's a goner," said Murphy, at Blake's elbow.

"Good God—I forgot her!" Blake swung around. "Rosie— her stand's at the end of the damned thing! And the kid's gone. She came to tell me something about it—"

"Better get up some standees," warned Murphy. "This is plumb hell and getting hotter. I'll keep things in shape here."

With a shout to four of the men, Blake leaped for the dock edge. Here they set up standees to hold the heavy tips and butts; it was burning hot here. As they worked, a hoarse tooting from the water announced the other two fireboats, nosing in with ladders and towers ready.

DIRECTLY OPPOSITE was a doorway, from which the door had been blown by the first explosion. It formed a wide frame for a murky hell within, drifting smoke shot athwart by flames. A faint popping announced tins of shellac and turps going off somewhere. Blake was turning up his coat-collar, when a gasp and a thump beside him showed Ironhead at his elbow.

"Better get a line in there," he said. "What about it, Ironhead?"

"Aye. Let's take a look."

PULLING HELMETS over their eyes to fend the heat, they dashed for the opening. Then Blake halted, gripping Murphy's sleeve.

"Look—for God's sake, what's that? See it?"

They peered. Something was moving. Something that fell and rose again. A small shape, a boy's figure.

"Rosie's kid brother, by God!" roared Murphy. "There, he's

down for good. Nobody can't get through that hell. What about it, damn you?"

"I can lick you at any game. Get a line up!"

All in half a dozen heart-beats, Ironhead Murphy was already roaring for volunteers.

"Two inch-and-a-half lines, there! Four men—keep us wet down. Move, blast you!"

The lines, charged but shut off, came up, and four men clumping with them. Blake was in through the gap of hell on the jump, with Ironhead plunging after him. Voices were megaphoning from the boats, ordering all hands back. Flames seared the air like shrapnel bursts as shellac tins exploded.

Blake tripped and went down, almost on top of the boy's limp form. He clutched it, and Murphy yanked them up. The streams of water played on them, around them, then stopped as the men at the lines were forced back. Clawing at each other and the boy, the two burly figures staggered out, tongues of flame licking the air greedily behind.

"Aboard the boat—everybody!" shouted Blake through blistered lips.

High time, too. The other boats were backing out of the firetrap of a slip. The boy was dropped aboard, Murphy and Blake scrambled after. The pilot let out a blast with the whistle-cord, and axes sheared the mooring lines.

"Half over to starboard!" yelled the pilot at the mate. Three more blasts. "Hold her!" And the *Viking* came out of the spouting inferno under full-speed bells....

An hour later, in the dingy office of Engine 72, Rosie Vidiano sat with the boy inside her arm. Chief Evans himself sat at the desk. Murphy and Blake, still blackened and freshly bandaged, stood listening.

"Then George the Slav is still in there?" demanded the chief quickly. As the boy nodded, he flung a glance at Blake. "That explains everything, huh? I guess there'll be no more anonymous letters and no more firebug work—hey, Jimmy! You say you saw him set the thing ablaze?"

Jimmy nodded eagerly. "I knew he was up to something, Chief. He had a boat under the pier, and when he went up, I snuck along and came up the ladder after him and took a look. He had a basin with scrap rubber and a lot of paper around it. Looked like he poured gasoline into it. He set a block of wood floating in it, with a candle on the wood, and lit the candle. I seen what was up, and let out a yell at him, and the hatch came down on me and knocked me silly. When I woke up, there were flames all around and I couldn't get down through the hatch, so I came on up through it and worked loose my sleeve that was hooked on a nail, and set off through the warehouse to find a door—"

Almost incoherent with his own haste, Jimmy exhaled a deep breath and started in again, but nobody was listening. Chief Evans had turned to Blake.

"Report at headquarters in the morning, Blake," he said. "I guess we'll talk it over and make up for lost time. Murphy, you did a good job tonight."

"Aw, hell, chief!" said Ironhead. "I didn't do nothing. It was this mug here." He jerked a bandaged hand at Blake. "It was my day off. He was acting cap'n. I hope to hell I aint going to lose him now."

CHIEF EVANS glanced at Rosie Vidiano, caught the look she exchanged with Blake, and his lips twitched.

"I guess you've lost him already, Murphy."

"Yeah?" Murphy turned, eyed the two, and nodded. "What about tomorrow, Blake, and them shiners you promised me?"

Blake met his eyes, and suddenly put out a hand to the bandaged hand.

"Ironhead, you said a mouthful a while back: Fire comes first. Tomorrow's another day—shake!"

Rosie Vidiano hugged the boy, her eyes shining.

# ONE MORE HERO

*A stirring story of fireboat men in action by*
*the able author of "Doghouse Blues."*

S ENIOR PIPEMAN and Acting Captain Lawrence, otherwise just Cap'n Lawrence of the fireboat *Ajax*, hated two things with a bitter and glowing hatred: one was heroes; the other was honorary fire chiefs.

"Blast it!" said Cap'n Lawrence at eleven o'clock. "I'm fed up with this!"

It was midsummer, with humidity at a point which warned of spontaneous combustion in the holds of nitrate and cotton ships; of explosions in grain elevators; spot fires in lumber-yards, flare-ups in oil-refinery stills, copra-reduction plants and oil-soaked fish-canneries. It was midsummer; for a solid hour Lawrence and his men had been at work alongside the wharf, for the benefit of an honorary fire chief, at orders of Chief Mason of the Fireboat Division.

Fifty kids strung out along the dock, attended by several teachers—Japanese, Mexican and Filipino tots from the fishing village at the end of the harbor. They were in charge of a tall, long-nosed pedagogue who wore an honorary chief's badge. And Cap'n Lawrence was fed up.

He clambered down the extension ladder from the griddle-like roof of the dock shed. A grueling drill, the firemen still on the ladders eighty feet above the wharf. Lawrence thumbed the sweat from his brow and glanced significantly at Chief Mason. The Chief took the hint. He made with his hands the gesture that meant "Pick up and go home!" in fire-department lingo. Immediately Lawrence turned and sang out aloft.

"All right, pick up!"

Chief Mason's red buggy moved off, followed by other cars bearing the visitors. The firemen were sending down tools and equipment from the flat roof. Lawrence eyed the odd-looking gadgets, so indispensable in modern fireboat work—breathing apparatus, smoke-masks, extinguishers, Siamese connections, reducers, adapters, reduction valves. A growl came from his massive throat, as he saw it all stowed away.

"Long and tiresome drills. A pumping exhibition—all six pumps started, and the boat swung out into mid-channel. Twenty drenched firemen, a dozen nozzles smeared with salt water, a good six hours of cleaning and shining deck bright-work. And all for a batch o'kids who don't know a fireboat from a mud-scow—and a long-nosed blighter with a badge!"

He drew a deep breath and shrugged. After all, it was life! Anyone with political pull could get an honorary appointment as assistant or battalion chief; and some took it seriously. A cheap and shoddy business, for these birds had to be treated with respect, all of them.

Lawrence set men to washing down decks and shining brass-work. He detailed others to unlimber and grease the big deck-guns—giant water monitors capable of delivering twelve thousand gallons a minute. Others went aloft on the water-tower to look after the top-turret, which must be ready at any instant to combat fires in the holds of ships high out of water, or in fish-canneries and oil-refineries beyond the dock sheds. Like many of his men, Lawrence had come out of the navy to go into fireboat work; and, a Naval Reserve officer, he did things navy style.

When the fireboat had at last been backed into her slip, he stepped to the wharf and headed for the office. Near the door, he paused to light a charred pipe. Honorary chiefs, indeed! Well, it was part of the job to play ball with them, or have

trouble. His eye touched on the sturdy lines of the fireboat, with complacent pride. Husky, six feet two, massive of build and muscled to match, Dave Lawrence looked what he was—one of the best men in the force, an Ajax to match this boat of his in power.

EVERY MAN, however, good or bad, has at least one spot in his past that he would give much not to see uncovered. And Dave Lawrence, with the most impeccable record of any man in the service, a man utterly devoted to his wife, a man whose wife was utterly devoted to him—Dave Lawrence was no exception. He alone knew of it, however. The wound had long since healed over, but the scar remained to torment him.

He knocked out his pipe. The pipe was an atom in that fist of his, that fist which balled to the size of a small ham. He turned and walked into the office.

*"—Captured by narcotic agents—"*

"Hello, Cap'n Lawrence! I was looking for you," said a harsh voice.

Momentarily blinded by the change from bright sunlight to this interior, Lawrence blinked. He did not know the voice or the man. A rather thin man, small, with a seamed face that was too old for the rest of him, bright eyes glinting from it, and a general air of knowing assurance.

"You don't remember me?" said the visitor. "I met you last year, when I was covering the waterfront for the *Herald*. Jim Nixon is the name. I got a newsservice of my own, now, and been waiting quite a while for a chat with you."

"Reporter, huh?" grunted Lawrence.

"Nope; that's in my dark past. Next time you have a ship fire, I want to go down in it with you. Got to get a story out of it, and other things."

Lawrence shook his head. "Nope. Nothing doing—"

"Hold on." Nixon drew back his coat, to display a police

captain's badge, and the gold badge of a fire chief. "Maybe these will persuade you."

"My God, another honorary chief, huh?" Lawrence bit off the words. "I suppose I got to humor you, and to hell with the taxpayers, huh?"

"Right," said Nixon calmly.

Lawrence flushed. "I do not," he said belligerently. "I'll do no such thing. Anyhow, we're not having any fires."

"A fortune-teller told me you'd be likely to have one today or tonight," said Nixon slowly, his eyes bright on those of Lawrence. "She even told me where it'd be—Berth 37, East."

"A fortune-teller!" Lawrence guffawed. "If you could pick out fires ahead o' time, feller, you'd be a wiz!" His laugh died out. His heavy brows drew down. "Berth 37? There's no ship lying there, wise guy. That's a Jap line pier."

"Yeah," said Nixon dryly. "So I hear."

SOMETHING IN the raucous voice pricked Lawrence. He came alert.

"You're interested in fires, aint you?" went on Nixon. "Fires in the holds of Jap cotton and general-cargo ships. You have four or five nasty ones every year. Smolders in piles of matting and cheap Christmas junk. Poorly stowed cargo. And you know as well as I do, just how accidental some of those fires are."

"What are you driving at?" shot out Lawrence harshly.

"Just that I believe in fortune-tellers, Cap'n, and I aim to be at Berth 37 tonight, and go down in the hold to see the fire. I'll go down with you."

"You blasted monkey! I've just told you there's no ship berthed there. If there was, you'd have to have a written order from the Chief before—"

"Nope," cut in Nixon, and flashed his badges again. "These are enough."

"They are not! I don't know whether you're a hophead or what—"

"I said, these would be enough," Nixon repeated. "Suppose I let you in on something?"

"You'd better not. You'd better scram before I kick you out," said Lawrence. "I'm a Government man as well as fireman; Naval Reservist, bound by oath to report any crooked work. And if you're not crooked as a dog's hind leg, I'll miss my bet!"

Nixon laughed easily. "Nonsense! Who ever heard of a newspaper man being crooked, Cap'n? I'm just curious. I want a story on the next fire. I like stories, queer stories. I've been working on one for a whole year, and now I've got it all clear. Maybe you'd like to hear about it?"

"I would not," snapped Lawrence. "I don't like anything about you."

"But this is a real human-interest story," Nixon said. "And maybe you knew the man. You must have been in the navy about that time—four or five years ago, it was. This chap was a petty officer. Quite a fighter, he was. Once in a while he'd light out and take another name and clean up some ham bruiser. No harm in that. He was working for a commission, and didn't want his fight activities known, but he needed the money. And one time down in San Diego he fought under the name of Kid Saunders."

"Never heard of him," Lawrence said throatily. The ruddy color in his cheeks ebbed.

Nixon lit a cigarette and went on.

"This time, Kid Saunders hit too hard. His man was a lumberjack from up in Washington—Frenchy Dubois, he was. Frenchy died two days later. Nothing was done about it; the fight was clean. But it worried Kid Saunders a whole lot. Stayed on his mind. He found that Frenchy had left a sister, see? His ship went into the yard at Bremerton, and he looked up Frenchy's sister, trying to help her out. He had a terrible conscience, Kid Saunders had. Of course, she never dreamed he was the man who had killed her brother. They got to be friends, and finally they got married."

NIXON PAUSED to drag at his cigarette.

Lawrence said nothing. He was making slow work of filling his pipe; under beetling brows, his eyes were intent.

What Nixon read in those eyes brought a slow smile to his seamed features.

"It's taken me a long while to run down all that yarn," he resumed, "but now that I've got it, I dunno whether to publish it or not, Cap'n. Might make trouble for that man if his wife found out, eh? A lot o' trouble! Besides, it might go on his record; might spoil him for promotion and pension. I dunno much about those things. What d'you think?"

"I dunno," Lawrence said huskily.

"Too bad. You see, I'm the only one who knows the story." Tossing away his cigarette, Nixon rose. "I'll be seeing you tonight, if that fortune-teller told the truth." With a grin, he tapped his badges. "I guess these will be enough after all, eh?"

"I guess so," Lawrence replied huskily, and cleared his throat. "But if that story ever did get into print, this Kid Saunders would prob'ly go after you and wring your neck—hard."

Nixon chuckled. "Aint likely. That'd be two murders on his record. So long, Cap'n!"

With a wave of the hand, he drifted out to his waiting car.

Lawrence put down his unlit pipe and wiped sweat from his face.

Fortune-teller, huh? A fire tonight, where there was no ship. What was this crook's game? Why did Nixon want to go down with him? He could not figure it at all. As to those hold fires in Jap ships, he knew all about that end of it, for the thing was no secret to those on the inside. A fire causing a few hundred dollars in damage, all insured, was a small matter when thousands of dollars' worth of dope could be passed in through longshoremen, in the confusion.

He could figure all about Kid Saunders, though; he groaned at the name.

It had caught up with him at last; the secret worry of years

*"You see me up safe; that's
all you have to do."*

had now broken to the surface. His record? This was nothing
at all, in comparison. It was the thought of Alice that tore at
him. If she learned the truth, it would wreck her, no doubt of
that. He knew her so well, he loved her so deeply! Her grief for
the dead brother had been extreme. All these years, Lawrence
had meant to tell her the truth, but he dared not. The knowledge
would horrify her. It was one of those things far better left in
obscurity, to be made up for by loving tenderness. But now—

He sat a long while unmoving. The color slowly came back
into his face, and with it newly graven lines that tensed about
his mouth. At last he drew a long breath, and reached for his
pipe, and lit it. He picked up the newspaper at hand, and tried
to put away the struggle in his brain.

THE NOON hour was past when Lawrence dropped the
paper he was still reading. He stifled the exclamation that rose
to his lips, then looked again at the shipping-news item which
had caught his eye. A Japanese freighter, the *Taku Maru*, was
due in this afternoon or evening and would berth at Pier 37,
East—

Lawrence scooped up the outside telephone and gave a number. A voice replied.

"Coast Guard Base, outer harbor."

"Hello! This is Acting Captain Lawrence, fireboat *Ajax*. Take a message for Commander Boone, to be delivered immediately. Here it is: 'Bad oil spill in the inner harbor. Send oil-pollution expert and intelligence officer over here this afternoon.' Got it? Thanks."

He hung up one receiver and took down the other.

"Lawrence, *Ajax*," he informed the fire department operator. "I want permission to make a practice run to Berth 37, East. Looks like fog tonight, and the pilot wants to check his compasses…. O.K., I'll hang on."

Permission was granted. Immediately Lawrence punched in a general alarm, using the ticker button over the desk.

A harsh clangor resounded through the barnlike structure. In less than a minute, the *Ajax* was steaming full speed out into the main channel, her crew climbing into their heavy canvas turnout coats, unreeling hose, fitting nozzles, making full preparations.

"Hold it!" Lawrence sang out. "Practice run."

"Where to?" demanded the pilot, who was surprised at nothing the fire captains did.

"Berth 37, East. Wanted to run some compass courses, didn't you? I told the Chief you did, anyhow."

"Sure!" The pilot was glad of anything to break the monotony.

"Then make it fast," said Lawrence. "Check fog courses and times, and also see how quickly we could get alongside 37 if we had a fire there."

"Aye." The pilot jammed the telegraphs down to "Extra Full Speed." The *Ajax* surged ahead and the mate steadied on the first course.

The long hot day came to an end. Everything bright and glittering, the *Ajax* lay in her slip again. All hands had settled down to an evening of chess and card games. They were hard at it when, at eight-three, a long ring came in.

"A still, sure!" exclaimed some one, as chairs overturned and all started for the boat. "A go, sure!" With a yell and a scramble, all twenty men were aboard, awaiting the word to go.

IN the Captain's office, Lawrence listened to the unhurried tones of the operator at headquarters dispatching-board.

"Berth 37, East, and stand by. Jap freighter *Taku Maru* arriving with fire in No. 2 hold. Chief says be ready with everything. Fire's under control, but may flash when hatches are removed. Got it?... O.K."

Lawrence hung up. "Fortune-teller?" he murmured. "Fortune-teller, my eye!"

The sixteen-thousand-ton freighter, with her port side forward shedding paint from the concentrated heat below and behind the steel plates, was pushed into her berth by three tugs. The *Ajax*, with all six pumps chugging, went alongside and was secured for a protracted visit. Her water-tower was raised; ladders shot up the hot sides; and booted and helmeted men started up with hose lines. Other men, already on deck from the land companies, hauled up the equipment from the fire-boat's deck.

"Hurry that breathing apparatus!" sang out Lawrence, who had gone up first of all.

Aboard the *Ajax*, men dragged out the boxes containing the smoke apparatus and the lighter smoke-masks. On the big freighter's deck, firemen unbent hitches and broke out the masks.

The breathing apparatus, a metal frame which held bottles of oxygen and "cardoxide," breathing-bags, regenerators, and other gadgets, weighed forty-eight pounds. Strapped to a man's back, which it more than covered, it was unwieldy; with a loaded hose and heavy brass nozzle, plus spanners, an ax and a first-aid kit, it made a man look like an overburdened Santa; but no man was allowed into a gas- or smoke-filled hold without it. The lighter smoke-mask was worn in front,—over the chest,—but was only good for half an hour in smoke, while the breathing apparatus could sustain life for at least two hours.

"Give me that apparatus," Lawrence shot at a fireman. "You, Bill, and you, Smith, rig out with me and stand by for orders from the Chief."

The heavy breather was strapped to the broad back of Lawrence; the metal helmet was fitted, the chin-strap secured. The mouthpiece and breather were inserted and tested twice. After final adjustments, Lawrence walked toward the hatch to wait until Chief Mason ordered the hatch-covers off.

BY THIS time it was pitch dark, and the ship's kingpost lights flooded the decks with yellow brilliance. The chief ordered the hatch-covers off; firemen lowered the fireboat's flood-lights into the smoke-filled hold. Lawrence inserted his breather-tube and fixed the wishbone nose-clips. He started for the iron ladder, but the Chief stopped him with a pat on the shoulder. Turning, Lawrence found himself face to face with Nixon.

The gentleman of the press wore a white fire-helmet with triple gold horns on the shield, the gold letters proclaiming him Honorary Assistant Chief; he also wore the identifying white slicker, and had on heavy firemen's boots. Chief Mason said, with a scowl of annoyance: "Lawrence, I believe you're acquainted with Honorary Chief Nixon. He says you'll take him down; he wants a story for the papers. Something like that reporter who broadcast his experiences from the bottom of the harbor in a diving-suit."

Lawrence undipped his noseguard and ejected the breather. He started to speak, caught the eye of Nixon, and with a short nod adjusted his breather again. Chief Mason turned to the watching men.

"Dress this man in a smoke-mask, go over the lifeline signals with him, and give him final instructions."

Nixon was led away. Chief Mason turned to Lawrence with a growl.

"Sorry, but you know how it is with these blasted honorary chiefs; orders are to handle 'em with kid gloves. Watch this guy, see he don't get into trouble. Maybe his newspaper yarn will do the department some good. Hero stuff, you know. Don't do any harm to let the public know what they pay taxes for, occasionally; they think all that firemen do is play handball and polish the seat of their pants."

Lawrence grinned. "Hero stuff!" He knew well the hollow mockery of that! The papers never got the tenfold heroic stuff that was pulled off day after day in the mere line of duty. By all means let the credit go to these pet honorary chiefs who needed it!

Longshoremen wearing gas-masks were now making ready to go below and salvage cargo not damaged by fire and chemical. And what a lovely graft that was, thought Lawrence with hard cynicism. Firemen had taken position around the hatch with nozzles ready. A word from the Chief would deluge the hold with tons of salt water from the bay.

The tarpaulins and wooden hatchboards came off. A bluish haze, loaded with deadly nitrous oxide, carbon monoxide and carbon dioxide, uprose on the night air. With it came the stench of charred matting and baled goods. Veteran firemen nodded knowingly to one another. They knew what lurked below—fire, assuredly, and death to the unwary. Woe to the man who lost his breather or nose-clip while fumbling around in the smoky darkness!

Abruptly appeared a squat, bullet-headed Japanese with four gold stripes on his cuffs—the skipper of the freighter. He singled out Chief Mason and bowed. "No water, plis-s," he hissed, motioning toward the battery of brass nozzles.

"What?" exclaimed the Chief. "If there's fire below, Cap'n, we must use water!"

"No water, plis-s," repeated the skipper, his black eyes like agates despite his mechanical smile of courtesy. "Valuable cargo, yes-s. Water would damage much. Use chemical, yes-s! We use all our own chemical. Fire under control two days. Smolder now, no danger. Use no water, plis-s!"

Chief Mason knew all about the cargo, though he had not seen the ship's manifest and cargo plan. He had got one whiff of the nitrous oxide. Down there would be a jumbled assortment of gimcracks made from celluloid and other such stuff, paper lanterns, oiled-silk raincoats and umbrellas. The smoldering goods would flash like gunpowder when sufficient oxygen from the topside got down to them.

Yet, for the moment, the Chief must agree. With the Japanese flag flying aft, the skipper was on his own soil and immune to foreign orders. So long as the fire did not threaten to spread, he could dictate the methods of fighting it.

DURING THIS interchange, Nixon, now accoutered, came up beside Lawrence and caught the latter's arm. With a glance at the half-hundred men—firemen, reporters, dock guards, longshoremen, Customs men and others—grouped around, he spoke quietly:

"I want to get into the upper 'tween-decks, next the bulkhead, to port of the manhole leading down to the lower 'tween-decks. The fire's in the lower decks, which the longshoremen haven't opened up yet. Never mind gamming about it. I know!"

"You know too damned much all around," grunted Lawrence to himself.

CHIEF MASON had started down the hold ladder on the opposite side, followed by four masked firemen with the long, rubber-insulated CO-2 nozzles. The men with the water-hoses had been ordered not to loose their streams except on direct order from the Chief; the little Jap captain, standing by the hatch, nodded approval.

Nixon adjusted his mask like a veteran, climbed over the hatch-coaming and descended into the smoke-wreaths. Despite his bulky apparatus, Lawrence followed as nimbly, dragging a chemical line with him. Firemen leaned anxiously over, tending the life-lines and signal-cords, which might mean life or death to the men below.

In the first 'tween-decks, Lawrence found Nixon standing under a ventilator outlet. Blowers were at work, and the air was pure here. The gases were rising up the hatch trunk from the smudge down below. Nixon had removed his mask. Lawrence pushed aside his breather and caught the smaller man by the shoulder.

"Listen, you monkey! So dope's your game, is it?"

"The less you know, the better," came the raucous voice. "You see me up safe; that's all you have to do."

He departed. Lawrence watched him beyond range of the floodlights, then inserted his oxygen breather and put on the nose-clamps. After making the proper adjustments, he left the ventilator intake. Nixon, scurrying like a rat, was worming in and around boxes and bales, his flashlight shifting quickly about.

What this was all about was only too clear. Nixon had known about this fire before it happened, and now knew exactly where he was going, and why. The fellow was one of a gang, of course; longshoremen or others would be in on it. And if Nixon squealed—Lawrence shrugged uneasily and indecisively.

Glancing back to the illuminated square of the hatchway, he saw that longshoremen were sending up the hatchboards from the lower 'tween-decks; soon the smudge below would get ventilation from above—then look out! The longshoremen, husky fellows with masks, were working hard in the glare and smoke. Chief Mason's white helmet flashed; the Chief was wearing a light smoke-mask, and so were the four firemen standing by with the chemical hose.

The last of the wooden hatchboards was lifted and sent aloft. Almost instantly, black smoke swirled up from the lower decks. Chief Mason motioned to the four firemen, who dived below in search of the angry red glower awaiting them. Lawrence's duty was to join the Chief at once, now the actual fire had been

located; yet he hesitated. He turned forward, and hesitated again. Nixon was working at something there.

With an angry oath to himself, Lawrence swung around and started for the hatchway. Duty prevailed; happen what might, he must go to his place. And at this instant, there came a dull roar from somewhere below. A flash of red flame upleaped; the dreaded back-draft had occurred. Lawrence, holding his hand before his face, retreated. Black smoke mushroomed up the hatchway; more bright flames mounted; an ominous crackling filled the hold. Air from above had fed the smolder with the necessary oxygen, and the result would be roaring flames that only tons of water could subdue.

Suddenly Lawrence staggered under a crushing blow on his neck, below the helmet. Dazed, half stunned, he went to his knees, was aware of a figure behind him, and whirled around as he rose. A giant of a man was there, in coveralls and a fireman's turn-out coat. Lawrence, sucking at his rubber breather, was into the vaguely seen figure with both fists, only to find

*Lawrence,
bewildered,
incredulous, fighting
blindly, was rushed
and toppled; another
paralyzing blow
to the back of the
neck dropped him.*

another dim shape charging in from one side. A third and fourth joined in. Lawrence, bewildered, incredulous, fighting blindly, was rushed and toppled over. Another paralyzing blow to the back of the neck dropped him. Kicks finished him in short order, and left him limp and senseless.

The four attackers played flashlights through the murk. One of them stooped and deliberately removed the clips from the nose of Lawrence, then groped for the main bottle valve to the oxygen. He shut the main valve, then the emergency bypass valve, making it impossible for Lawrence to get oxygen, even had the breather been between his lips.

A fifth man joined the other four. Then, with a rush, they joined the firemen and longshoremen who were madly climbing for the topside and safety. Looking exactly like the others, they merged with the scramble and gained the decks above. Another instant, and at Chief Mason's command, the firemen around the hatch let go with the water.

A shrill whistle brought Lawrence to himself.

Still dazed, bewildered, gasping, he sat up with a jerk. The whistle persisted. It was the alarm on the breathing apparatus, warning the wearer that his oxygen was low or his bypass valve closed.

Mechanically, Lawrence reached down and opened the valve. He gulped a stinging breath of smoke and gas, and automatically reached for his nose-clip that dangled on its safety string. He clamped his nostrils shut, inserted the rubber breather between his lips, and began to suck straight oxygen into his burning lungs.

AFTER REPEATED efforts, he heaved himself up from between the bales that hemmed him in; the cumbersome apparatus strapped to his back seemed to weigh a ton. Only half conscious of his movements, he found his main bottle-valve and opened it; this switched him from the straight oxygen to a mixture, and made his breathing less labored.

Another dull explosion came from below, and with it, the roar of the deluge that the fire-nozzles were directing into the inferno. Sucking at his breather, exhaling laboriously into it, Lawrence staggered out of the recess among the bales. The clumsy apparatus weighed him down intolerably; but to part with it was sure death. His brain reeled; his head and neck ached; his flashlight was gone, and he could see almost nothing through his fogged goggles. He turned toward the trunkway and the ladder that meant safety, only to check himself with a low and bitter curse: Nixon!

His brain cleared. The entire queer and illogical affair flashed into exact focus; he saw it all on the instant. Nixon was one of a gang, yes, but had attempted to double-cross his friends and get away with the dope himself. Lawrence had been aware from the first that a gang was at work. Now he saw where Nixon came in. But—when he himself had been downed by the gang, what about Nixon?

TEMPTATION TORE at him, hesitation belabored him. If Nixon had been caught, it was none of his affair. If Nixon, like himself, had been left to die, what harm? That rat's death would solve his own problems.

None the less, he staggered back into the darkness, feeling his way through the labyrinth of freight. He knew where he had last seen Nixon. With a groan and a curse, he headed for the spot. It had to be done. Duty spurred him with relentless prongs.

Another explosion sounded below, and the hold became a raging furnace. The boxes of paper lanterns and celluloid toys had gone up like gunpowder. On deck, Chief Mason met this new challenge by ordering the top-turret of the fireboat to work. The six-inch pipe, with pumps hammering behind it, was trained below; and together with the other nozzles, the *Ajax* was now delivering her full capacity of twelve thousand gallons per minute. Soon the fire would be out, and the hold would become a thirty-foot well filled with floating debris—with two men at the bottom of it....

The firemen stood grimly intent at their posts. The Chief had vetoed all offers of volunteers to go below and look for Lawrence and Nixon. Suddenly a yell went up, then a mad chorus of voices. The huge, smoke-blackened figure of Lawrence was descried struggling up the ladder. On his back was the breather, and draped over the apparatus and about his massive neck, dangled the limp form of Honorary Chief Nixon.

Slowly Lawrence fought his way up the searing iron ladder, until others leaned down and relieved him of the dead weight. A wave of delighted yells broke out, as Lawrence was pulled over the coaming; he collapsed amid the helping hands.

H E   C A M E  to himself as the rescue squad finished bandaging his hands. He sat up, his bloodshot eyes blinking around. Firemen, longshoremen and reporters were all around him; flashlight bulbs were clicking. Lawrence pressed his bandaged hands to his singed brows, with a grunt.

"What happened?" he demanded.

"That's what we want to know," replied a newspaper man. "Come on, give us the yarn! Nixon never did amount to a hang, but it's a great story. What happened?"

"Yeah, come clean!" put in another man. "This is hero stuff, you bet!"

Lawrence coughed. *Hero stuff!* The word wakened him warningly, brought caution into his brain. He blinked at the men around, and licked his sore lips. Yes, he could give them a real story if he wanted to do it; but he knew better.

Suddenly a grin twitched at his lips; he turned it into a grimace, uttered a groan, and sank back with closed eyes. The rescue men bent over him with restoratives; he sat up again, coughing.

"Never saw anything like it," he muttered. "Greatest piece of nerve I ever saw—say, where's Chief Nixon?"

There was a little silence. "You got him up all right, Lawrence," said some one. "Too late. The gas had overcome him. Nixon's dead."

Lawrence stared at his bandaged hands. Nixon was dead!

"It's a shame," he said at length huskily. "Dead! Well, boys, in all my time at sea I've never seen such nerve. I'll tell you, all right. He and I were looking for the smudge in the upper 'tween-decks. It was dark down there, and I led the way, see? Nixon was behind me. All of a sudden I stumbled, lost my flashlight, and fell. An open manhole with the lid up. Down I went into a trunkway or something—about ten feet, I guess. I hit bottom, landed on the back of my head, and went out cold."

He paused. The newspaper men were intent, scribbling as they listened. Another flash-bulb popped, and Lawrence blinked.

"Next I knew," he went on, "Nixon was shaking me. My nose-clip was off; the breather was gone, and I'd taken in some gas. Nixon worked like a horse. He lifted me, rigged my nose-clip and breather again, and began to haul me up that manhole ladder. I helped all I could, but was still half out. How that little guy ever got me up that trunk, I dunno; but he did it.

"He got me up the ladder and over to the hatchway. There was an explosion; flame beat up. It must have burned through

*Slowly Lawrence fought his way up the searing iron
ladder, until others leaned down and relieved him.*

our signal cords and life-lines. I went out again, but Nixon
fetched me around with an inhalant from his first-aid kit. There
was another explosion, and the concussion knocked me off my
feet. When I got my bearings, I couldn't find Nixon. I went
back among the cargo and found him lying face down, his mask
off. From then on, I just don't remember much, boys. I made
fast to him, and that's all."

"Great Scott!" exclaimed some one. "It was you who brought him up!"

"Don't remember it," said Lawrence, shaking his head. "Anyhow, that was nothing. It was Nixon who pulled me out of that manhole; I'd be in the gas and smoke right now, except for him. It took nerve, boys—real nerve! And you say he's taken the long count? Gosh, I'm sorry for that."

Lawrence wiped an eye that was red enough for actual tears.

"Give him the credit, boys," he went on earnestly. "It was no job to get him up the hatch. Think of his pulling me out of that trap—me weighing two hundred and twenty without a breather on! That's what killed him—overtaxed his heart, I bet you. He was all in after he pulled me out. I should have known enough to give him a stimulant, but I was woozy after that fall and the gas. Well, you know how it is—"

They knew how it was, all right. What a story! An obscure and none too creditable member of the Fourth Estate, a voluntary fireman, braving smoke, gas and roaring flame to rescue a brother fireman, paying with his life for that bit of valor—what a story!

NEXT MORNING, when Lawrence read that story as he sat in bed, he grinned widely. He was given only passing mention, and his wife was highly indignant as she brought him his coffee. The telephone rang, and she answered it, then turned.

"It's Commander Boone," she said. "If you're not able to get up—"

"Huh? You bet I am." Lawrence whipped out of bed and sat down at the telephone.

"Hello, Lawrence! Read the paper yet?"

"Just got it, Commander. I was reading the Nixon story—"

"Oh, that! Well, you read the story on Page One, second section," came the reply. "And say! That Nixon story was a hot one. I never knew you were such a high-class liar. I'll be around sometime today, and find out what actually happened."

"Okay, Commander; I'll be here," said Lawrence.

Page One, second section? He reached hastily for it. A flash came into his eyes; no mention of him here at all, naturally. But an account of five men who had mingled with firemen and long-shoremen and gone down in the burning hold:

> —captured by alert narcotic agents as they were leaving the pier. In their possession was what officials estimated as pure heroin worth $150,000. It is believed that this capture breaks the back of the narcotic ring which has for years been flooding West Coast ports with—

"So they got 'em!" thought Lawrence, laying down the paper.

His mind went back to that moment in the office when he had listened to Nixon's threat. He had sat there alone, sweating blood; but in the end he had put in that call to Commander Boone, and damn the consequences!

"By gosh, I come mighty near being a real hero myself!" he muttered. "Only—thank God, nobody knows it. And never will."

His wife bustled in. "Are you going to drink that coffee or not?"

"Yes'm," said Acting Captain Lawrence meekly. "That is, if you sweeten it right."

She did, with a warm embrace and a smile. Then she pointed to the newspaper.

"They want you to appear at the funeral of that man Nixon tomorrow, dear," she said. "So take it easy today."

"You bet I will," said Lawrence. "His funeral, huh? Yeah. I'll be there with bells on. Didn't he save my life?"

# FIREBOAT STYLE

*They eat smoke and drink flame and handle an*
*excursion-boat fire at sea—all in fireboat style.*

KANE SAT in the boathouse galley that morning, eying the men around over his pipe and listening to their profane grousing. The crew of the fireboat *Typhoon* were mugging up while awaiting the presentation of their new captain, and there was trouble in the air. They were, undeniably, a bad lot.

Kane was the only man aboard who was here by reason of merits, not of demerits. Uptown he was Cap'n Kane; he signed himself *Ed. Kane, Master*, or *Edward Kane, Lieutenant, U.S.N.R.*, according with whom he did business. But here at his job aboard the fireboat, he was Pilot Ed Kane, pilots being picked only from the ranks of ship's masters.

As Kane could see with half an eye, Bill Magill was going to be a storm-center when the new fireboat captain showed up. Senior Pipeman Magill was tall, angular, ungainly, and the homeliest man in the department; also the ablest trouble-maker, between fires.

"Cap'n Whalen, the boy wonder!" he sneered. "Eight years from clodhopping to skipper in a metropolitan fire-department! Eight years. Now he's cap'n of the *Typhoon* and all the other rigs at this here Back Channel station. Aint it lovely!"

"It's great news, if you ask me," said Tom Connell, chief of the engine-room gang. "You swabs have been needing some one with a prod."

Kane chuckled. "Yeah?" he cut in, cocking an eye at the chief engineer's red corncob nose. "He'll have his work cut out to wean our prize bottle-baby!"

Connell glared, but with a twinkle in his eye. He and Kane knew how to give and take and still remain fast friends.

"Is that so?" he retorted. "Next time a certain pilot raids my locker, I'll wean him with a spanner! Deck-swabs better stay out of my engine-room."

The crew, all misfits culled from uptown truck and engine companies, took sides, some for Magill, some for Connell and his Irish whisky. Actual battle impended, as it did all too frequently—until three sharp, sudden rings came on the alarm extension.

The fifteen staring, glowering, sulky men lined up on the apparatus floor. Old Battalion Chief Coyne introduced the new captain in his cracked voice.

"Boys, this is Cap'n Bob Whalen, your new commanding officer. I want you to get in and hit the bell for him same as you always do. And I don't want any reports from him about any of you. The first man he turns in to me, goes straight to the main office."

That was Joe Coyne's stock warning, and no one heeded it. The Chief stalked out, got stiffly into his red coupé, and was whisked away, with Whalen seeing him off. The crew waited for the coming fireworks. They had already taken Whalen's measure, and he had taken theirs at a glance; and both of them were very largely correct.

Kane, who could make allowances for both sides, waited uneasily for Whalen's return. By virtue of his position and character, he was safely out of the war; but he resolved to risk trouble by trying to make Whalen see some light of reason.

Engine Sixteen, the official designation of this fireboat and its hose-tender, foamite and combination rig, was located in an abandoned fish-cannery in the oily deadwater at the head of the Channel, where the smelly shrimpers and Sound oysterpungeys berthed. Men were hard to handle at Engine Sixteen; it was a post of tough citizens.

Captain Whalen strode briskly in. With a nod to Pilot Kane, who was in the crew but not of it, he faced his hardbitten outfit. He was no angel himself. A trifle above middle height, massive-jawed, black of eye and brow, he looked assured and arrogant in his neat uniform. He fingered a notebook, scanned the unhandsome faces, and spoke in quietly imperative tones.

"Men, the *Typhoon* faces a new deal. It may be painful. I'm familiar with the service records and the personal peculiarities of every one of you. I know why you're here. But I know my duty and responsibility. In future, we turn to at eight sharp.

Come on duty shaved and breakfasted. Be in dungarees at eight o'clock line-up; from line-up, go directly aboard the boat.

"No mugging-up in the galley after eight; and no Kaffee Klatches at ten, as you've been accustomed in the past. Meals at regular hours; no man will absent himself from the boat or station except by my permission. I call your attention to Headquarters Bulletin No. 47, December second, 1937, about drinking on duty. If a man shows up drunk for muster, or even with the smell of liquor on his breath, he goes at once to the Chief at local headquarters."

Whalen drove a significant glance at Marine Engineer Connell. Some one down the file snickered. Whalen's sharp eyes went straight to the culprit.

"No more of that. You, third from the end—what's your name?"

"Magill," sneered the lanky troublemaker. "George Magill,— Bill usually,—senior pipeman, fire-tug *Typhoon*, Berth Eight."

"Senior pipeman no longer." Whalen's voice was razor-edged. "Senior janitor in quarters till you learn to say 'sir' when replying to a superior officer."

Magill's gray eyes blazed; the others stood aghast. A new deal with teeth in it! Magill had nineteen years on the job; for ten years he had been acting captain when the regular skipper took his days off. Longer than Whalen had been in the department!

Magill had superior knowledge of the hazardous waterfront, an uncanny ability for sizing up a fire and going into action without lost motion, and reckless courage; but he was an incurable ribber, and bitterly quarrelsome.

He remained ominously silent; a glance at the sullen faces of the others, and Whalen dismissed them curtly. Slowly the crew broke ranks and shuffled away. Magill, Pilot Kane and Chief Connell were called to the Captain's office; and there Whalen eyed them, before addressing Magill crisply.

"I regret that you chose to be antagonistic. For your behavior in ranks you get two months as houseman. I warn you that your station must be in first-class shape for ten-o'clock inspection each morning."

"And I warn you," burst out Magill, "that you're riding to the hardest fall anyone ever got!"

"As I remember my notes on the crew," Whalen said without emotion, "you have fifty demerits. Another thirty will automatically let you out. If you utter one insubordinate word in the future, out you go. That's all."

Magill shambled out. Kane started to speak, but checked himself, He was a rough-hewn man, harsh of feature and voice, with twenty years in the coastwise lumber trade.

Whalen turned to the Chief.

"Your record as an efficient engineer is A-1, but your reputation as a secret drinker while on duty, is bad. The attitude of my predecessor toward your faults was disgraceful. I'll report you the first time I find you under the influence of liquor."

Under this broadside, Connell scratched the end of his red corncob nose.

"And I warn you, Cap'n," he said in his whisky-husky voice, "that you've bit off more'n you can chew. When you get in a bad jam, you'll learn what it means to have the crew ag'in' you."

"Meaning they'll lay down on me and cause me to lose a fire?" barked Whalen. "If I catch any man shirking, I'll file charges of cowardice and see him on the street minus his badge!"

"You'll likely go with him, sir." Connell grimaced. "I've been thirty years right on this old boat. I've seen cap'ns and crews come and go. Them that go ahead o' time, go because they don't realize one fact: Waterfront fire-fighting is like nothing else on earth. There's a lot to learn that drill-towers or engine-work uptown won't teach a man."

"It's no secret that this crew are the most shiftless gang who ever slipped by an examiner," said Whalen with contempt. "Not one of them got higher than C rating when I had them as drill-master. They'd not last a single shift in any uptown company."

"Throttle down, Cap'n," advised Connell, still rubbing his battered nose. "If you're bound to give 'em the works, taper it off with easy doses."

"I'll be the judge as to that," said Whalen. "I have a free hand; the Big Chief uptown will back me up."

"Yeah; I knew the Big Chief when he was a rookie," observed Connell. "He's had some fine fires uptown, but down here among the canneries and fishboats and sulphur plants and fish-net storehouses—"

"Old stuff." Whalen rose abruptly. "A fire's a fire."

"But there's different kinds o' smoke," said Connell shrewdly. "We can eat as much smoke as any fancy uptown truck- or engine-man, but between fires we take it easy. When we work, we take extra risks. It's no joke, fighting ship fires.

"The worst fires, Cap'n, are the ones in ships, outside the breakwater. It gets rough out in the Sound; and when a ship's engine-room has been gutted by fire, the ship can't maneuver to help the fireboats."

Whalen was interested, but too stubborn to admit it. He did not intend to invite this notorious old souse to sit down and offer advice.

"We don't get called to fight fires outside the harbor," he said. "We have two new boats, faster and better equipped—" He broke off, at Connell's grin. "Well? What's the joke?"

"Nothing much, sir. Nothing except them new boats are gas-boats—the devil's own invention. All right when they run, but give me a good triple-expansion engine with Scotch boilers, for a long haul and hard work!"

"And a bottle of Scotch to keep yourself oiled?" snapped Whalen.

"No sir! A bottle o' prime Irish."

"That'll do for today," Whalen broke in. "Remember what I said at line-up! Leave liquor alone while on duty."

"Aye, sir. And remember we'll have ship fires like we've always had—and when the new gas-boats are laid up, most likely!"

Connell departed, taking his thirty-year-old distillery aura with him. Whalen turned to Kane, with a nod.

"Glad to have you with me at least, Kane."

"Thanks. I'm afraid you're off to a bad start," said Kane, regardless of the hard stare his words evoked.

Whalen bristled. "Sorry you've taken that attitude, Pilot Kane. When I want your advice, I'll ask for it. That's all."

TWO MORNINGS later the old chief showed up for duty under the influence of his favorite tipple. One minute after line-up and muster, Whalen had the battalion chief on the wire. Chief Coyne heard him with dismay.

"But, Whalen, we can't turn old Connell in! He's been thirty years on the job, with never a mark against his record. Never on the sick-list, even!"

"Right now, he's under the influence," Whalen pointed out crisply. "I warned him particularly. If he gets away with this, I'll never have any discipline. I'll make out the report now and send it over by the assistant chief, who's on his way here. It's my right, and I request you to send the report in to Headquarters through proper channels."

Coyne could only curse under his breath, and assent.

Two days later Connell came down to the fireboat and sorrowfully removed his gear. He shook hands with the scowling crew, the ominously silent pilot, even with Captain Whalen, and departed without a word. Thus began the new deal on the *Typhoon*.

MAGILL, ERSTWHILE acting captain and senior pipeman, was next to feel discipline. A fish-net fire was carefully set by a fish-boat crew who had enjoyed a poor season and needed the insurance-money on their expensive nets. The *Typhoon* responded. Being first in, by all the rules of the business she was expected to cover exposures, then lead in to the fire.

Magill, to whom this was an old story, expertly sized up the fire as the boat drew in alongside the wharf and the shed of fish-nets. Quite forgetting the new captain, in the heat of excitement, Magill gave his orders before Whalen could catch his breath.

He sent two men ashore with a two-and-a-half-inch hose to cover other small buildings near the burning shed. Four more firemen he sent ashore—two with another hose line, two with a twenty-foot extension ladder. The last pair placed their ladder, mounted to the shed roof and began to chop a hole for ventilation. Magill himself was on the business end of the hose with the first pair, leading the way with helmet reversed into the shed.

Another captain might have stood aside, kept his mouth shut, and watched. The fire would have been out in two minutes. But Whalen, feeling himself purposely ignored and humiliated, sharply recalled the men from the roof before they could chop the essential ventilating hole. He also pulled Magill and his two men out with their hose.

"What the hell's the big idea?" snarled Magill, his face streaming sweat and blackened by smoke. "Going to let the works burn?"

"I'm in charge here," Whalen said sharply. "Take that nozzle, go to the east side and break in a window or door. Take your line in from there as you should have done. I'll hit it from this side." He turned to the other men. "Lead in with the $CO_2$ nozzles, one man to the nozzle!"

At his shout, a man on the $CO_2$ platform amidships cracked the first three of the carbon-dioxide bottles in the series. Men unreeled the copper hose, now flooded with the gas, and four returned to the smoke-filled shed.

"You priceless sap!" yelled Magill. "It takes water to put out net fires, water and overhauling!"

Whalen swung around. "Pick up that nozzle and get around to the east side!"

*"I warn you," burst out Magill, "that you're*
*riding to the hardest fall anyone ever got!"*

"Pick it up yourself and go to hell!" rasped Magill.

The Captain went white.

"You refuse to obey a lawful order at a fire?"

Magill glared at him. "I'll work for no numskull. You're no fireman. Any rookie would know this is a job for lots of water and overhauling. You send men in there to be overcome by their own CO2 gas as well as smoke. And you've lost the fire; it's the first three minutes that count."

Magill was right. The storeroom was gutted, and ten thousand dollars in nets destroyed. Battalion Chief Coyne came storming up and blared at Whalen to haul out the CO2 lines

*"If you utter one insubordinate word in
the future, out you go. That's all."*

and hit the fire with water. Magill, standing idly by, grinned
sardonically; but his grin faded when Whalen reported him for
insubordination and refusal to obey orders. The Chief suspended him on the spot, and the suspension was later verified
at Headquarters; Magill, awaiting trial, joined Chief Engineer
Connell on the bench.

THE REST of the crew, anticipating that their turn would
come, gave the new captain plenty to worry about.

They never shirked; instead, they moved faster and apparently worked harder than ever before; but when they reached
a fire, everything they attempted was bungled. Ladders went

up swiftly, but something always happened when men started to take up the lines. A twenty-foot extension would collapse; hose would fall from firemen's hands; axes and other equipment were lost; hose burst under excess pressure or became hopelessly entangled, was often burned.

In a word, when the *Typhoon* arrived at a fire and was first in, she created such confusion that the action of the other boats and the land companies was hampered, and valuable time was lost. This was sabotage; Whalen and the harbor chiefs knew it, but at fires accidents may happen to the best-drilled companies. Also, the crew of the *Typhoon* carefully had their accidents when Captain Whalen's attention was elsewhere.

The skipper was baffled; he was totally unable to pin anything on any one of his men. Here was a case where the advice and regulations in the Rule Book were worthless. He retaliated by putting on pressure and living up to the rules by letter. The men responded as men will. They did their work, but only when he was watching, and then poorly. He worked them from eight to six. Chores were usually caught up by noon in the department, but he kept them at tasks when the other crews were at cards or handball.

Conditions grew worse. Whalen became morose and kept to his office. He was jittery; when an alarm came rapping in, he would jump a foot. Behind his back the crew jeered silently. No one spoke to him unless addressed; they were giving him the silent cure. When he came upon groups talking or smoking, they dispersed.

Too late, Whalen changed his tactics. The men were fighting among themselves now; old feuds were rekindled, hatreds burst into flame. None the less, when he became affable or took sides, they dropped everything and gave him the cold shoulder. One dark night they let him pump a burning fish-boat full of salt water and sink her, when he could have saved her with a few pounds of carbon-dioxide dry extinguisher.

Events in all fire departments have the habit of shaping

themselves up swiftly and unexpectedly, long periods of idleness varying with prolonged and sustained effort almost superhuman. Whalen could not smell the future as Pilot Kane did. Kane felt sorry for the man, who meant well. He saw that Whalen was bewildered, dared not ask for a transfer, could not ask that any of his crew be transferred. Kane said nothing; but inwardly felt that a showdown was coming. A sense of desperation grew upon him.

He learned that old Connell was laid up, too old to get a job. Magill got one, but promptly lost it for fighting. They never came near the boat, but the news did. Kane boiled—it was all so useless!

AT PRECISELY two o'clock one afternoon the fire-phone rang. Captain Whalen, working over time reports, scooped up the phone with no premonition that fate had struck.

"Fireboat *Typhoon,* Cap'n Whalen—yes sir! What's that?"

For twenty seconds Whalen frantically jotted down instructions from the battalion chief; then he kicked his chair back and punched the relay button overhead, sending the long, shrill alarm through the old building. Grabbing hat and turn-out clothes, in another twenty seconds he was joining the crew on the fireboat.

Everything happened now, not in minutes, but in split seconds.

While boiler furnaces roared under forced draft to build up a capacity head of steam, Pilot Kane, in the wheelhouse, scanned a large-scale chart of the Sound. He laid dividers on the chart, tapped the barometer above the chart table, and swore under his breath. A falling glass, westerly winds hauling to the north, storm-warnings flying from the breakwater pilot station—and the ancient excursion steamer *Saxby City* afire, fourteen miles to the north!

Aboard the steamer were two hundred excursionists returning from the Island after the last picnic of the season. Kane knew the picture. Fourteen miles the *Typhoon* must fight her way through heavy seas against a growing gale. And aboard her were fifteen malcontents, unable properly to extinguish a fire on a forty-foot yacht in a quiet harbor. Bitter need now of old Connell at the engines!

For an instant Kane felt fearful tension; he had the mad, blind impulse to kick Whalen overboard and do what must be done. Two hundred lives at stake—good God! What mattered his own record, pension or anything else, in such a gamble? Then he suppressed a groan as he saw Assistant Chief Roy Bright, of the Marine Division, come stamping aboard the boat. Bright had been driving close by when his car radio picked up the alarm. He was another landsman, and this was sea business. Bright, too, was the wrong kind. Kane saw Captain Whalen meet Bright, and bring the latter to the wheelhouse with him. In barged the first mate, gangling Jim Foster, like Kane an ex-coaster in the lumber trade. He came close to Kane and spoke under his breath.

"Hey, Ed! Got a grapevine from Bill Magill. Some one passed him the word about the *Saxby*. His niece Sally is on the old hooker, in charge of a lot of orphans. Bill and old Connell will be at the end of Pier Six about the time we pass."

Kane nodded. With this, the die was cast; he knew it, accepted it.

"Get going!" roared Captain Whalen. "The *Saxby City*, afire off the Bay!"

"Take it easy," advised Kane calmly. "Nothing to be alarmed about." He sounded a long blast on his whistle, put the engine telegraph on half-speed ahead, and the *Typhoon* shot out from her slip.

"Hell of it is, that we have to send this old tub on such a run!" said Chief Bright disgustedly. "Two new boats able to make eighteen knots; and that damned pilot on the *Deluge* would have to pick up a wire hawser in his propellers, while the *Monsoon* would naturally be in dry-dock. *Arrgh!*"

PILOT KANE smiled grimly, his eyes intent on the Channel entrance ahead. He swung the annunciators to full speed and gave an extra jingle. The *Typhoon* trembled and surged as the engineer who had replaced Connell fed steam to the ancient engines.

Both new boats laid up! Captain Whalen thought of old Connell's prediction, but did not mention it; to practical, seasoned firemen, the expected rarely occurs, the unexpected is always around the corner.

The fireboat, her siren warning all small craft to keep clear of her wash, plowed down-channel. Abruptly, Kane swung the annunciators to *Stop;* the mate twisted his wheel to port. *Full*

*"Sally is on the old hooker," Foster said, "in charge of a lot of orphans."*

*Astern! Stop*—again. Four bells and a jingle ahead, and they resumed their course.

It all happened so swiftly, was done so deftly, without a word between pilot and mate, that the assistant chief and the Captain were taken completely by surprise. They did not know why the abrupt stop had been made, until suspended fireman Magill and suspended engineer Connell came to the wheel-house. Magill ignored the officer and spoke to the pilot, briskly.

"Engineer Connell and Fireman Magill reporting to the master for duty!"

Kane glanced over his shoulder. "Aye," he said, as though it were all regular. "Find a B Division man's gear in the nozzle-room, and get ready for tough going. You know all about the construction of the *Saxby City*. Get the gang together and dope out what you'll do if the fire's for'ard, amidships, aft or in the engine-room. Connell! Take your old place below. Tell Squires I sent you, and get two more knots out of those engines."

"Aye, Skipper!"

THE TWO men grinned, and climbed down the ladder as though unaware of the officers standing speechless. Chief Bright suddenly came to life with a bellow.

"You can't pick up suspended men and put 'em to work! Kane, have you gone crazy? Turn in at Pier *22* by the pilot station and land those two men. Quick!"

Kane turned a beaming face to them.

"This is the greatest piece of luck that ever was! With those two fellows aboard, now we have an even chance—"

"Do you hear me?" roared Chief Bright. "Land those two men at Pier 22!"

Kane, with a grin, kissed berth and record and pension good-by.

"Gentlemen," he said politely, "step inside my room; find seats and take it easy. I'm master here, subject to U. S. Department of Commerce rules. You may wear a dozen badges, but you've nothing to say aboard this boat."

"Another insubordinate, eh?" burst out Whalen. "I've been expecting this; you've just been waiting for the moment to start something. This will finish you, Kane!"

"Maybe not," Kane rejoined. "Suppose you read Section 27 of your ever-ready Rule Book. Captains usually skip that section. It's about fireboats and pilots."

"Stop this nonsense!" erupted Chief Bright, purple in the face. "Kane, will you obey my orders?"

"I will not; it'd be a criminal waste of time, sir." Kane calmly faced forward. "Jim, port a little! Cut inside that day-mark and head straight for Number Three bell-buoy—there! Steady on."

"By heavens, I'll file charges! I'm in command here!" stormed the assistant chief. "You're a subordinate, subject to my orders, Kane. I'll have you suspended for this!"

Kane flung him a grin. "Look in my room, sir. There's a red book on the shelf called 'Law of the Sea;' it'll instruct you. Once we cast off moorings, I'm master of this ship, with absolute authority. I'm out to save the people aboard the *Saxby City*, and I don't give a damn what you do tomorrow; but if I have any interference from you today, I'll chuck you over the rail—so chew on that. You'll find it more comfortable in my room, by the way. We're going to have it rough."

The Assistant Chief and the Captain turned into the bunk-room abaft the wheelhouse. Kane exchanged a grin with Jim Foster, and then looked outside the breakwater, where mountainous seas were building up. Already the fireboat was lifting and rolling to the swell, and taking spray over her blunt bows.

Well, it was done; and Kane felt better about it. For good or ill, he had the bit in his teeth now. It had been forced on him. Department discipline had gone to blazes, and his future with it—but he was glad.

ONCE OUTSIDE, the boat made heavy work of it. Kane, beside the annunciators, watched the dripping bows rising and plunging again. Black smoke poured from the funnel, to be snatched to shreds by the whipping wind. A blast of sleet rattled viciously against the windows.

Kane cursed the operators of the *Saxby City*, who should have laid up the old steamer for the winter long ago. Some of the City Fathers had persuaded them to give an excursion to orphans and wives; to make the trip pay, the operators had loaded the old ship with cargo, against all regulations. As though answering his thoughts, the ship-to-shore radio, silent since the departure, burst into action.

"Calling fireboat *Typhoon*, fireboat *Typhoon!* Radio operator on *Saxby City* has his dynamo running again. Fire in fore part, in the mail room, under temporary control. Two hundred bales of hay from Port Lambert; drums of varnish and raw linseed oil from West Hanlon refinery. All forward, forehold and lower passenger-deck, temporarily housed in. One hundred eighty-two passengers, women and children, quiet and orderly; crew under good discipline—"

Followed a repeat, a break, and more information.

"Navy sending two destroyers from north Nimrod Sound, two Coast Guard cutters from Point Gibson station; should reach *Saxby City* one hour after *Typhoon*. Fireboats *Deluge* and *Monsoon* should arrive about the same time. That is all for present."

Pilot Kane cursed again. Two hundred souls, a ship afire in a gale; hay, linseed oil and varnish stowed below, instead of on deck where it could be jettisoned! Some one would lose his ticket, but the owners as usual would go scot-free.

Captain Whalen and Bright, hearing the radio, had returned to listen. Their features were the color of whey, and they were swallowing hard. Foster, the mate, had lighted a rank pipe and was puffing furiously. The two officers sniffed the acrid smoke, and gagged; abruptly they jerked open the wheelhouse door, and unmindful of the cold and drenching spray, staggered out on deck. Foster and Kane exchanged a look and a grin.

"Better take a glance aft," said Kane. With a nod, Foster departed, and after a moment was back, shivering.

"All O. K. Magill brought a quart of rum aboard; just enough for a hearty nip all around. Tom Connell's happy as a clam at high water, and drunk. He's got the safety valve screwed down two-blocks and his mills turning to capacity. Them babies are sure singing a lullaby for the old boy. Superior officers are jammed between the chemical bottles over the engine-room cuddy, looking into the bottoms of two fire-buckets and praying. I told Magill to cover 'em with salvage tarps when they were through pumping out their lunch."

THE *Typhoon* pounded down the gale-lashed sound. She was taking the seas like a duck, even though spray was going over her funnel. The wind increased each moment; sleet and snow beat against the windows, and Kane held her steadily to her course. Darkness, coming early with the storm, was upon her already.

Down below, old Tom Connell fed live steam to his clanking, whirring pets, making his rounds with grease-swab and long-necked oiler. Squires tended the furnaces and kept the burners free of carbon. Above all the bedlam of noise, the husky voice of Connell could be heard, roaring out a familiar chantey:

> *Eight bells and all's well,*
> *Cap'n and Chief can go to hell!*

The fireboat charged past Gull Inlet and Kane verified her speed by a bearing on the light. The ten-knot fireboat was making a good thirteen; she would reach the burning ship in a trifle over an hour. Kane relaxed and called Foster to the wheel.

"Flashing red light on the port bow." Foster handed over his binoculars. "Must be Oyster Pond bell-buoy."

Kane focused the glasses. "It's Pond light," he said with a nod. "I raise Placid Bay beacon a point on the starboard bow. Put her on nor' by east, nothing to the east. I hope old Sandstrom got into Placid Bay. It'll make our work easier."

*"These are the babies!"*
*yelled Magill at his men.*
*"Come on, you boys!"*

PLACID BAY was reached, but old Sandstrom had not got the *Saxby* inside. The rockets were going up now; they were close to their destination, and Kane swore feelingly with crisis at hand. Another rocket. Kane opened the port door and blew a blast on his pocket whistle. Presently Magill came lurching up the ladder.

"Work's cut out for us," said Kane tersely. "The *Saxby's* had to anchor outside, and we might as well be smack on the high seas."

Magill grunted and wiped salt spindrift from his eyes.

"Put us within jumping distance, and we'll get lines aboard her."

"I'll run up under her lee, if she has one. You give yourself plenty of scope on the lines so you won't part 'em." He broke

off abruptly and lifted his glasses. "There! The air's cleared—
there she is! Good God, look at her! It's broke out on 'em;
probably reached the hay and linseed oil. Damn old Sandstrom
for a careless fool! He should ha' refused that cargo in spite of
orders—"

The *Typhoon* changed course a bit and plunged on.

Magill roused the firemen out of the nozzle-room; they
began unreeling hoses, and preparing tips and nozzles and
heaving-lines; then they held on to anything handy and stared
at the spectacle ahead.

To any seaman, it was terrifying. The *Saxby City*, with her
twin smoke-pipes and ridiculous paddle-wheels, lay just outside
the Placid Bay whistle-buoy. Captain Sandstrom had put over
a stern kedge, and the steamer lay stern to the thundering seas;
good judgment there, for had he anchored with his bowers, the
fire forward would have swept aft and consumed the ship. The
steamer was now a flaming beacon, with the fire obviously
beyond control.

"Must have carried away his wheel-ropes," muttered Kane,
as he switched on the powerful carbon searchlight. "They
couldn't stand the whipping of the rudders in a following sea.
Too bad the mate didn't think to put on relieving tackles before
they started home!"

Wreathed in flame and black smoke which the wind tore
into long streamers, the old ship wallowed at the end of her
kedge-cable; the glare brought into mad relief the yeasty crests
of the seas pounding at her.

Suddenly new flames, fed by burning hay, began eating
farther aft with visible speed, aft toward the crowded ginger-
bread upper decks. The fire-tug seemed pitifully small and weak
in the downwind welter. Kane put the engine on *Slow Ahead*,
thrust his head from the wheelhouse door, and emitted a roar
at Bill Magill.

"Hey, Bill! I'm going to chance putting her in alongside,
for'ard. I may crash, but it's the only thing to do."

"Go to it!" shouted Magill lustily.

Cupping horny hands, Kane sent a shout at the two firemen in the top of the reeling, swaying water-tower thirty feet above the after-deck.

"You guys give it the works the minute we get grapnels into her!"

The towermen waved assent and limbered up the elevating and training gear.

Foot by foot the *Typhoon* crept under the lee bows of the flaming ruin. Wan as two anemic ghosts, Assistant Chief Bright and Captain Whalen emerged into sight. Too weak to do more than hang on to the chemical-bottle rack, they watched the *Typhoon* and her hard-case crew go to work. Rolling, taking green water over her bows, the fireboat edged up beneath the bows of the steamer.

KANE, HIS hard features dripping spray, his slicker long since torn to shreds, jockeyed the telegraphs and barked orders to Foster, wrestling with the kicking wheel as the wind whistled through the open windows. The bows, with their ragged rope fender scooping and shouldering aside the seas, at last touched the side of the steamer. As the fireboat lifted on a crest, a fireman on the slippery roof of the wheelhouse flung a grapnel with ten-foot chain leader attached. The iron gripped, held, and another man snubbed the hawser.

"All fast!" went up the yell, and the towermen loosed their deluge.

THE UPROARING flames, hit by two hundred and fifty pounds of pressure, subsided as by a miracle. The towermen at the controls heroically kept the monitor's long brass pipe trained on the fire; with the mad plunging of the two craft, it was a task. One minute the stream would be beating down from an acute angle, next it would be shooting upward.

The fire was checked, but not beaten. It ravenously attacked the lower decks and began to eat its way aft beneath the main deck. A sudden roaring explosion rocked the steamer, and new flame flared up. The linseed oil had been reached.

"Skipper!" Magill was swaying from the brass hand-holds, two steps below the wheelhouse. "We gotta get aboard! Can you put us flush alongside?"

"I'll try anything you crazy galoots will!" Kane shouted.

"Then it's alongside." Magill let go and reeled forward. His voice rasped out like a fog-horn. "Hi, you lardos, stand by to board! Two men each on the fog-nozzles, and never mind the metros. Stand by to jump when we close. And watch yourselves, you club-foots!"

Kane put the telegraphs on *Stop*, ordered the helm from hard astarboard to 'midships, and the seething waters flattened the *Typhoon* flush alongside the burning ship. The double-bow-lines with their steel grapnels held; Kane, to offset the tremendous scend of the seas, put the engines back on half speed.

Magill led off. When the plunging tug rose on the crest of a comber, he leaped and landed over the top-deck taffrail. He had bent a heaving-line around his wrist; with this he pulled up the chromium ten-foot fog nozzle and its trailing hose.

"Gimme plenty of slack!" he yelled back at the tenders. "And charge the lines when I get inside with two lengths!"

The heavy hardwood vertical fenders of the tug rasped the steamer's side. She rose on another wild sea; two more men with heaving-lines were safely over. Once more the *Typhoon* lifted on a hissing sea, and two more men jumped. Kane came out to the rail.

"Five's enough!" crackled out his voice. "Rest of you stay aboard and tend the hoses. Don't let 'em get pinched, either. Charge all lines! Hundred and fifty pounds!"

Magill was off with a wild yell, two men backing him up; they disappeared down a hatchway, straight into the smoke. Captain Sandstrom and some of his men worked forward and helped pull up hose. The other two firemen followed. Two ten-foot nozzles went wide open for the fire's heart.

Captain Whalen coughed and retched, and looked, from his place on the chemical platform. He cursed himself and his seasickness, as his eyes went to the two men in the plunging tower monitor, keeping that stream steady. He looked forward along the canting, water-spouting decks. Kane was first on one side of the tiny bridge, then on the other, jockeying the telegraphs and yelling commands at Foster, who worked at the wheel. Directly below him was the main engine-room hatch. Whalen looked down and saw old Connell, smeared with grease and sweat, keeping gaunt face and bloodshot eyes on the lettered disks of the telegraph. Signal bells clanged incessantly; the pointers jumped from one speed to another on a split second, as the pilot rocketed down his mechanical commands; unmindful of the sickening sway of the greasy floor-plates, of the wild tossing, of the stench of burned oil, Connell never made a false move, never bobbled a signal.

WHALEN LOOKED forward at the men lightening hose, bending connections, tending lines and fenders, while thunderous seas came tumbling over the bows. He turned and looked at Chief Bright, clinging beside him; the eyes of the two met and held.

"Tired of bein' sick, Bright?" demanded Whalen. "Up-and-coming officers, aint we—fine-looking men alongside of them misfits and incorrigibles!"

The biting sarcasm of his voice went home, brought the red to Bright's pale cheeks.

"Well?" he went on savagely. "Want to get your uniform dirty or not?"

"You crazy larrigan!" Bright straightened up. "I'm with you if it kills me."

Whalen coughed again, and plunged away toward the starboard gangway. Bright came staggering after. Two drenched firemen tending lines forward of the wheelhouse saw the two officers and stared. Kane, appearing at the starboard wing of the bridge let out a yell.

"Hey, you boneheads, you can't do that! Don't jump, I tell you—"

"Go to hell," gasped Captain Whalen, and jumped.

MAGILL, MEANTIME, was up against dense smoke and sheeted flame; when the fog-nozzles opened, the smoke thinned and the flame retreated.

"These are the babies!" yelled Magill at his men, thrusting the ten-foot nozzle ahead. "Come on, you boys, give it hell!"

The fog-nozzles, recently designed by some land fireman, had just come aboard, had been used at drills, but never at real work. Now they showed their worth. Foot by foot, Magill and his four men battled their way into the blazing compartment.

Through the six holes in the showerbath-like end, the water stream at a hundred and fifty pounds pressure was discharged like a heavy fog that lent a weird halo to the flames; the firemen felt little heat, as that flying mist penetrated and smothered the fire ahead. There was no whip or squirm to the hose, either.

"Hurray! This is something like! We got her licked!"

After twenty minutes of intensive work, Magill yelled exultantly. In the thick fog, his men were mere vague shapes. This lower deck, ordinarily used for passengers in summer, had been housed in to protect the cargo of hay from the sea. Water cascaded down from above, mingling with the spray and fog.

Magill trained his nozzle on a pile of smoldering baled hay, and let out another and wilder yell. The bales had actually been used to check off drums of paint and oil!

"Keep them drums wet down!" rasped his voice. "Bring over that two-and-a-half inch—spot that corner! Here, you, get in there—you with the yeller slicker, go topside and get cargo-hooks to overhaul this mess. Good job! Hit 'er again!"

A fireman who had been handling the floodlight, hauled over from the fireboat, came up and punched Magill in the ribs.

"What is it?" Magill turned furiously. "Gone nuts, have you?"

The man grinned and swung the bright glare of his light.

Magill forgot the heat and smoke and stench; there, laboring over tangled hoses, were Captain Whalen and Chief Bright. Both of them were sick and staggering, but they never slacked; they gave no orders, worked like common hosemen, and worked hard.

"Hurray!" Magill went to them, slapped them on the back. "You got what it takes, you two guys—you got what it takes!"

And surprisingly, the two grinned back at him....

An hour later, when the job was completed, the two officers were still at work. They sweated and labored, spat soot and coughed blood, choked and retched and obeyed the bailed orders of Senior Pipeman Magill until they could barely put one foot before the other.

With six searchlights converging on the *Saxby City*, a coast-guard cutter edged in and demanded to know what help was needed.

"None," sang out Pilot Kane. "We're casting off and going home. The fireboat *Typhoon* doesn't need help."

"You're damned right," added Bright, gripping the rail. "Send in that message and sign it Assistant Chief Bright, in charge."

Kane gave the wheel to Jim Foster, took Bright's arm, and headed him below. They halted before turning into the galley. Captain Whalen, blackened and grimy, was just accepting a cup of black coffee from Connell and Magill.

"It's ag'in' all the rules," said old Connell, wagging his head.

"Yeah," assented Magill. "No mugging up in the galley, says the book. No meals except at regular hours."

CAPTAIN WHALEN looked at the two of them.

"Hereafter," he said, "Engine Sixteen goes by the Book of Rules—fireboat style. I'd not be surprised if you two mugs found yourselves reinstated with merits, and all your demerits wiped out. And that pilot of yours—by the Lord, he's a man!"

Captain Bright nudged Pilot Kane violently.

"That goes for me, Kane," he said in a hoarse voice. "Damn

your eyes, you salute me ashore—and afloat I'll salute you, every time! Fireboat style, you bet; shake! And rules be damned. We're all men together, and that's the whole story."

# ABOUT THE AUTHOR

H. BEDFORD-JONES is a Canadian by birth, but not by profession, having removed to the United States at the age of one year. For over twenty years he has been more or less profitably engaged in writing and traveling. As he has seldom resided in one place longer than a year or so and is a person of retiring habits, he is somewhat a man of mystery; more than once he has suffered from unscrupulous gentlemen who impersonated him—one of whom murdered a wife and was subsequently shot by the police, luckily after losing his alias.

The real Bedford-Jones is an elderly man, whose gray hair and precise attire give him rather the appearance of a retired foreign diplomat. His hobby is stamp collecting, and his collection of Japan is said to be one of the finest in existence. At present writing he is en route to Morocco, and when this appears in print he will probably be somewhere on the Mojave Desert in company with Erle Stanley Gardner.

Questioned as to the main facts in his life, he declared there was only one main fact, but it was not for publication; that his life had been uneventful except for numerous financial losses, and that his only adventures lay in evading adventurers. In his younger years he was something of an athlete, but the encroachments of age preclude any active pursuits except that of motoring. He is usually to be found poring over his stamps, working at his typewriter, or laboring in his California rose garden, which is one of the sights of Cathedral Cañon, near Palm Springs.

www.ingramcontent.com/pod-product-compliance
Lightning Source LLC
Chambersburg PA
CBHW070942250626
47159CB00009B/3352